THE BEVERLY GRAY

MYSTERY STORIES

BEVERLY GRAY IN THE ORIENT

The BEVERLY GRAY *Mystery Stories*

By CLAIR BLANK

BEVERLY GRAY
IN THE
ORIENT

By CLAIR BLANK

GROSSET & DUNLAP
Publishers　　　NEW YORK

Contents

BEVERLY GRAY IN THE ORIENT

CHAPTER I

Fright

THROUGH THE DARKNESS came a scream and the tinkling of shattered glass.

"Pirates!" yelled Lenora Whitehill and pulled the bedclothes over her head. A second later she peered out and whispered: "Lois! Lois!"

There was no answer. Now fully roused, Lenora swung one foot over the side of the bunk and stood up. Her friend's bed was empty. Lenora looked skeptically at the door of the cabin.

Excited voices could be heard in the corridor, demanding why, what, and who was responsible for the noise. Snatching up a dressing gown, Lenora darted thither.

"What's up? Any pirates aboard?"

From one cabin came Beverly Gray and Shirley Parker. Across the companionway the group's chaperon looked out. Roger Garrett and Paul Benson were talking to Lois while Terry Cartwright and Jim

9

Stanton were on their knees on the floor picking up the shattered remnants of a drinking glass.

"Hold on, Lois!" Paul smiled. "Tell us exactly what happened."

Lois, whose face was white and frightened, shoved her hands into the pockets of her dressing gown and endeavored to grin. As she looked from one to the other of her friends, she ran a nervous hand through her curly hair.

"I came out to get a drink. I got it and was going back to our cabin when——" She hesitated and looked at the door at the farther end of the corridor which led to the storeroom down in the hold of the ship. "When," she continued, "a hand came round the edge of the door there——"

"A hand?" Lenora inquired laughingly.

"A hand," Lois repeated. "It was all full of red stuff. Blood it looked like, and——"

Lenora giggled unfeelingly. "It was that pineapple-upside-down cake you ate before you went to bed. I told you you would see pink elephants."

Roger jerked the door in question open and peered down the steps into the hold where the ship's supplies and excess luggage were stored.

"Not a sound nor sign of anyone," he said.

"You were dreaming, Lois," Lenora told her friend.

"But I wasn't!" Lois insisted. "I actually did see a hand."

Lenora tucked her arm within that of Lois.

"Come along back to bed."

"You think I'm crazy," Lois accused as she followed Lenora. "But I tell you I did see someone——"

"We might as well all go back to bed," Roger yawned.

The corridor was deserted as quickly as it had filled. Silence reigned until a slight squeak heralded the slow opening of the door into the hold. A pair of eyes peered out into the dimly lighted corridor. A figure slipped through the opening and cautiously tiptoed first to one door, then another, listening. Then, still cautiously, and with the utmost silence, he ascended to the deck.

"I suppose Lois was dreaming," Shirley Parker laughed as she climbed back into her bunk.

Beverly yawned. "Lenora will try to convince her that she was."

Beverly found that the incident of Lois' nightmare had thoroughly driven all thoughts of sleep from her. Try as she would, Beverly could not follow Shirley's example and go to sleep again. Finally, tired of tossing, she rose and dressed in sport clothes. She left the cabin without arousing Shirley and gained the deck.

She walked to the stern and stood by the rail, watching the trail of sea foam the yacht left in its wake. During the many days that had passed they had seen the lands of Napoleon, Caesar, the Pharaohs, had come past Rome, Athens, and through the narrow blue ribbon of the Suez Canal. Now they were in the Red Sea en route to India. The land of mystery and intrigue!

Readers of Beverly Gray on a World Cruise are already familiar with the first stops of the "Susabella." They will recall how Beverly, Shirley, and Lenora started out with Jim Stanton, Paul Benson, and Miss Ernwood on Roger Garrett's yacht. In England they had some exciting adventures when Jim came into possession of a torn map which they secretly hoped would lead them someday to a treasure. Beverly met a Count Alexis de Frachiny whom she discovered later was after the map. When they sailed from London Terry Cartwright had been added to their passenger list and in Paris, where Beverly received the news that her novel had finally sold to publishers in New York, they picked up Lois Mason.

Now Beverly lived over the events of the past weeks. Exciting times in Cairo where Lenora secured her prize scarab! She remembered the words inscribed on the back of the scarab: "Destruction to those who take from Egypt the things which are Egypt's." Whether the threat would mean anything to them they had yet to discover. Lois was in favor of getting rid of the scarab at the first opportune moment, but Lenora guarded it jealously.

Dawn was breaking over the east and the sky was beginning to be alive with colors. Beverly turned and paced the deck thoughtfully. In the bow she discovered Lois with a sketching board in her hand.

"Hullo," Beverly said in surprise. "I thought you were asleep."

"Couldn't sleep," Lois said. Her pencil was busy. "This is too grand a sight to miss."

"Think I'll get my typewriter," Beverly said. "The morning is inspirational."

Beverly descended the companionway to the cabin she shared with Shirley. There she picked up her portable typewriter and a few sheets of paper. She was starting to leave the stateroom when a scream rang out—followed by a splash.

Shirley awoke with a start.

Beverly had already dropped her typewriter and was running out into the corridor. There she bumped ignominiously into Jim.

"What was it? Who was it?" he cried.

Beverly raced up the companionway to the deck. "Lois is overboard!" she shouted over her shoulder.

CHAPTER II

Discovery

—————————————————————————————

By THE TIME Beverly tossed a life preserver to Lois, who was struggling in the water, the rest of the passengers and crew were on deck.

"Try to get any sleep on this boat," Lenora grumbled as she helped Lois establish herself in a blanket and deck chair. "Couldn't you wait for the rest of us to get up before you went swimming?"

"Swimming?" Lois echoed indignantly, striving to give Lenora a withering glance. "Somebody pushed me into the water."

Lenora and Shirley both laughed at that.

"Don't tell me the same bloody hand you saw downstairs pushed you off the boat," Lenora giggled.

"It did!" Lois declared.

"Woo Fang's pineapple cake is more potent than I thought," Roger grinned.

"What happened, Lois?" Beverly asked seriously.

"Yes, what did happen?" Paul Benson seconded.

14

"Well, Bev, you know I was sketching here on deck," Lois said.

Beverly nodded. "You were walking toward the rail as I went down for my typewriter. Then what?"

"Well, I hoisted myself up on the rail, leaning my back against the pole there." Here Lois stopped long enough to indulge in several sneezes. "I was sketching the distant shore line when I thought I heard a sound. You all know the door to Woo Fong's kitchen is right opposite to where I was. The door was slowly opening and I saw——"

"Well?" Lenora said impatiently. "What did you see? Don't tell me it was another bloody hand!"

Lois colored hotly. "If you think it such a huge joke——"

"Lois, please," Beverly said hastily. "What did you see?"

"A man," Lois said. "He had black hair, and his white shirt and hands were all covered with red stuff——"

"Are you sure?" Roger put in. "Had you ever seen him before?"

"I was so surprised," Lois continued. "He stepped toward me and put out his hand. I felt myself slipping backward and the next thing I knew I was in the water."

"Then he didn't actually push you in," Lenora said. "He just frightened you so that you fell. But who was he?"

The others looked at each other blankly.

"Are you certain you never saw him before?" Paul insisted.

Lois shook her head doubtfully. "I might have, but I didn't recognize him. With all that red stuff——"

"Was it blood?" Lenora asked, wide-eyed.

"It looked like it." Lois shivered.

"You have to get into dry things immediately," Shirley said, hurrying Lois away. "With those shivers you will be sick when we land in India."

The others straggled away to dress also. Lenora, having been dressed when Lois screamed, remained on deck with Beverly.

"Do you suppose she actually saw someone?" Lenora asked Beverly.

Beverly frowned thoughtfully. "She would scarcely have the same dream twice in succession."

"But if there is someone else on the boat where is he?" Lenora asked, casting a glance over her shoulder as if she expected to see the intruder rise up behind her.

"If you wanted to stow away on a boat where would you hide?" Beverly asked Lenora. "Not on deck in plain sight. Surely not even in the crew's quarters."

"I'd hide away where the provisions and excess baggage and such things are stored," Lenora said promptly.

"Exactly!" Beverly nodded. "Therefore, if there is someone on the boat isn't it logical to suppose he would be down in the hold with all—all our junk?"

"Lois said that is where she saw him first!" Lenora said excitedly. "Remember? The hand came around the door into the hold——"

"Let's go!" Beverly said.

The two darted down the companionway. Lenora disappeared momentarily into the lounge and reappeared with a flashlight which she found in a desk drawer. The two cautiously approached the door to the hold. They preferred to go alone, rather than with all the others. For one thing, if they waited, the man might disappear or do some damage. If they acted at once perhaps they could catch him off guard.

The light from Lenora's lamp danced over the steps below them. Its white glare cut the blackness like a flash of lightning. Beverly descended first while Lenora held the lamp for her. When she was two steps from the bottom she could see there was a huge wet spot of some dark substance on the floor. Lenora was beside her in a moment, examining it. Lenora tentatively stuck her finger into it and then regarded that bit of her anatomy in the glare of the flashlight.

"It's all red, Bev! It's blood!"

"Blood!" Beverly echoed laughingly. "Silly! Can't you smell it? It's paint."

"Paint?" Lenora said with a sheepish grin. "So it is! Red paint!" Her flashlight located an upset can beside the stairs. "The burglar or whoever it was must have upset the can on himself," she said.

"Right!" Beverly agreed. "Look!"

"W-what?" Lenora inquired. "Footprints!"

The girls bent eagerly over the prints on the floor, prints very discernible because they were made of the wet sticky paint. Lenora kept her light trained on them, and they followed the prints for several paces. In the center of the floor they suddenly stopped.

"That's funny," Lenora said. "He couldn't have vanished into thin air. What happened to him? There isn't anything close enough for him to hide in without taking some more steps."

Beverly was examining the footprints closely. Now she spoke up. "The footprints were made by rather heavy shoes. When he got here they stop. So——"

"So what?" Lenora demanded.

"The man must have discovered he was making prints and taken his shoes off."

Lenora made a wry face. "There go all our clues! Now what do we do?"

"Search the place," Beverly said, straightening up. "We must make sure he isn't hiding in any of these boxes or an old trunk or something."

Meager threads of light were beginning to stream in through the portholes. These, together with Lenora's flashlight, gave sufficient light for the girls to see what they were doing. Empty cartons and crates were examined, dark corners explored, every conceivable place was investigated.

"Look over in that corner, Lenora, and then we will have looked everywhere," Beverly said wearily.

Lenora crossed to a corner filled with crates of foodstuffs. Carrots and cabbages and cans of this and that, together with several huge sacks.

"Potatoes," she said as she looked into one of the sacks. "Nothing here, Bev."

"Then let's go up and get some breakfast," Beverly proposed.

"That is the best thing you've said this morning," Lenora declared heartily.

When they gained the lounge the others greeted their appearance with various shouts and laughs.

"What in the world were you doing?" Shirley demanded. "Look at yourself—all smeared with dust."

"We were looking for Lois' man of mystery," Lenora said. "But we did not find a thing." She took her place at the breakfast table. "Gosh, am I hungry!"

"As usual," Terry Cartwright laughed.

The others were equally eager to devote themselves to the tasty dishes placed before them. When breakfast was over Woo Fong, the Chinese cook Roger had brought along especially for this voyage, appeared in the lounge and bowed low before the young master of the "Susabella." He had been a servant in the Garrett household for many years and liked his young master very much. Now his round, moon-shaped face was wreathed in smiles.

"May have word with Mista Logah?"

Lenora always enjoyed the cook's English. He had

the usual difficulty with his r's, and his pronunciation of Roger turned out to be "Logah."

"Certainly, Woo Fong, what is it?"

"Extla special cake allee same disapleah."

Lenora giggled. "Lois, you ate too much last night. Woo Fong, we certainly did make that cake disappear!"

Woo Fong shook his head. "Many blead and cheese and sandliches disapleah also."

"Bread, cheese, and sandwiches too?" Roger said in surprise.

"Who was walking in their sleep last night?" Lenora demanded.

"The man Lois saw!" Beverly and Shirley exclaimed together.

"He came from the kitchen," Lois agreed.

"But where did he go and how did he hide all that stuff?" Jim wanted to know.

"We all rushed to the rail when Lois was overboard," Terry put in. "He could have come through the door into here and gone into any of the cabins unseen."

"Oooooooo, maybe he is waiting for us to go to sleep," Lenora said in a hushed voice, albeit her eyes twinkled mischievously, "then he will murder us and take command of the 'Susabella.' "

"Rot!" Terry said crisply. "But I say, we had better search the boat now."

"I agree!" Paul said. "No telling who he is or what he is doing aboard."

"Woo Fong make more cake?" the cook wanted to know, grinning.

"Make two cakes," Lenora implored. "One for us and one for the burglar."

The young men went off purposely to systematically search the ship, Lenora and Lois trailing after them offering advice and looking for excitement.

When the young people left Jerusalem shortly after Christmas, they had gone down through the Suez Canal into the Red Sea. Except for a short stop at Jiddah in Africa, where they had seen the Tomb of Eve and taken on a few extra supplies, the boat had not loitered at any port. How a man could board the boat unknown to them was a mystery. How he could remain hidden was more of a mystery still.

"Well?" Shirley asked eagerly when first Lenora and then Lois and the boys started to straggle wearily back to the lounge. "Did you find anything?"

"Nary a bug," Lenora said. "He must be a ghost."

"Ghosts don't eat sandwiches and things," Lois said scornfully.

"How do you know?" Lenora countered swiftly, laughingly. "Have you ever been a ghost? Have you ever asked one what he ate? Have you——"

"I'm going to sketch for a while," Lois said, rescuing her dignity and going up onto the deck.

"And I'm going to write," Beverly said determinedly.

The day passed leisurely. Beverly and Lois devoted the major part of their time to their respective arts.

Terry and Lenora had a really strenuous game of ping-pong; strenuous because when Lenora hit the ball no one ever knew where it would land, least of all Lenora herself. Shirley and Miss Ernwood for the most part read magazines. Roger and Jim and Paul spent their time repairing the radio.

After dinner the radio did double duty, for the young people kept it going constantly. It was an attraction after being out of order for several days. They danced upon the deck to the lilting music that came from the loud-speaker.

It was ideal dancing in the cool air with only the moon, stars and one Chinese lantern to light the deck. Lenora teased Terry to teach her to tango, so the young man finally succumbed and the others were interested spectators. Roger and Shirley sat side by side on the wicker divan. Paul and Lois stood at the rail. Beverly lay in a long deck chair while Jim sat on a hassock at her side.

Beverly leaned her head back and sighed with pleasure. It was such a happy group here. They traveled together in perfect harmony, through fun and danger, through familiar sights and strange. They had come a long way from the day they set sail in New York. Halfway across the world! Beverly thought of the typewritten pages lying below in her cabin. A story for Charlie Blain, the managing editor of the *Tribune*, who had given her her first job. Now that her book had sold (and what a thrill she got every time she thought of that!) she had no rest until she could write another. But meanwhile she wrote short stories for the *Tribune*.

"Bravo!" Lois applauded Lenora and Terry.

"Aren't we good?" Lenora grinned modestly.

The dancing became general again and lasted for quite a while, until a fine, stinging rain, coming up suddenly, drove them in off the deck to find their beds.

Beverly didn't know how long she had been asleep, but quite suddenly she was wide awake. She had the queer feeling that something, or someone, alien was in the cabin. She could hear Shirley's deep, regular breathing. Her friend was still asleep. Beverly lay perfectly still, listening and straining her eyes into the darkness. Not a single beam of moonlight entered through the porthole. The cabin was all an inky blackness. The throb of the mighty engine echoed in her ears; she could hear the swish of water as the boat plowed through the sea. Every sound was magnified tenfold.

"Imagination!" she told herself sternly and tried to go to sleep again.

From the deck came the silvery tinkle of the ship's bell. The pillow was soft and cool against her cheek. She was comfortable but sleep had entirely fled. In imagination she already walked beside the Taj Mahal, rode an elephant through India's mighty jungles, and sailed on the muddy Yangtze River in a Chinese junk. She thought eagerly of the mail awaiting them in Bombay. In the last letter she received in Jerusalem from Connie Elwood she had promised to mail Beverly a copy of her own book as it came from the New York presses. Now Beverly was impatient to see her brain child. She sighed. It was delicious to be idle, drifting with the tide toward adventure and unknown scenes, knowing that a future was being built for her with each sale of her book. In high school and college days she had dreamed, never thinking that she might be actually doing it, of the places she would visit someday.

What was that? Without moving, Beverly listened intently. A board creaked again. It was not one of the accustomed sounds of the ship in action. This seemed to her more like the stealthy step of an intruder and it was close to her! A sudden dim flicker of moonlight through the open porthole let her see a vague shape outlined near her trunk. Who was it? Her heart beat pleasurably fast. The long-sought burglar? If Shirley were only awake! She would need help to catch him. A sudden run for the door would net her nothing. He could escape easily before Jim or Roger or any of the crew could be roused to come to her aid.

Another slight sound and Beverly knew the intruder was on his way toward the door. What would happen if she screamed suddenly at the top of her lungs? She smothered a giggle. She would scare Shirley out of five years' growth—but she would also scare the burglar and wake her friends. Tentatively she reached out a hand toward the dressing table.

It closed around a jar and her exploring fingers came
in contact with cold cream. She took a firm hold
and when a splinter of light showed for an instant,
as the intruder looked out to make sure the corridor
was clear, Beverly threw the cold-cream jar and
screamed loudly, at the same time grabbing a dressing gown and jumping from bed.

The jar of cold cream splintered against the door
a scant inch from the burglar's head. Shirley woke
with a smothered cry. Beverly dashed into the corridor in time to see the intruder disappearing up the
companionway. Doors opened as excited occupants
tumbled from warm bunks to demand what was the
matter.

Roger and Jim dashed after Beverly as she went
up to the deck. A dark figure was climbing over the
rail. The three Americans ran to the rail but they
were too late. The figure dropped to the water and,
as they watched, climbed into a rowboat waiting and
pulled away from the yacht. As they watched, a hand
was waved in salute.

"Who was he?" Roger murmured. "What was he
doing on board?"

Beverly shook her head and did not answer. Her
thoughts were confused. In the brief glimpse she had
had of the man, she could scarcely believe her eyes.
Was it possible? Could it have been the man she had
known in England and Switzerland and France as
Count Alexis de Frachiny? Perhaps she had been only
half awake and her imagination running riot, but so

it had seemed to her. The fleeting glimpse she had had, she was sure, was of his black hair and slight, wiry figure.

"Where are the Indians?" Lenora demanded, stepping out onto the deck. "Ooooo, it's wet and cold! Terry, who yelled?"

"It wasn't me this time!" seconded Lois.

Shirley straggled after the other two girls while behind her came Roger's aunt with Terry and Paul.

"Somebody certainly messed up our cabin," Shirley volunteered. "Were you playing football with yourself, Bev? Is that ice cream dripping from our door?"

"It's cold cream," Beverly answered. "I threw it at the burglar. He was looking for something. Look." She pointed out over the water. "There goes our mysterious intruder. He had his boat waiting and hopped into it the minute we discovered him."

"I wonder if he got what he was looking for," Lois murmured.

"Jim," Beverly said suddenly, "do you still have the half of that map Slim gave you in England?"

Jim plunged his hand into the breast pocket of his pajama coat.

"All safe and sound, why? Do you think——"

"I think that fellow was Count Alexis," Beverly said.

"What?" the others shouted.

"I'm certain of it," Beverly said more firmly. "I wonder how he got on board."

"If he intends to row back to France he has a long pull ahead of him," Lenora giggled.

"We're only a few miles from Aden," Roger said. "He is probably heading for there."

They straggled down to their cabins again. The more Beverly thought of it, the more convinced she was that it had been Count Alexis in search of the half of torn map Jim had in his possession. Beverly remembered how persistent the bogus Count had been in France and Egypt. He had been determined to secure the map for himself. So determined, in fact, that the young Americans became suspicious and decided to keep the map and see what made it so valuable. Too, if they could secure the second half from the mysterious person named Black Barney, perhaps they could discover the treasure the map was supposed to indicate.

CHAPTER III

India

INDIA! Excitement ran high as the white yacht neared the front door of India—Bombay. For days they had scanned the horizon for sight of land—the long-awaited and eagerly greeted land of India!

"What do you think of when you think of India?" Lois asked as they all stood at the rail watching the dock draw closer and closer.

"Elephants and snake charmers," Lenora said promptly.

"Ruined temples," added Shirley.

"The Taj Mahal," Beverly chose.

"The hunting trip Terry is going to take us on," Roger said.

Sir Terence Cartwright, known familiarly as Terry, was proving a valuable addition to their world party. He had wired to a friend in Bombay and that friend had immediately put his whole house at their disposal while they were in Bombay. It would be exceedingly more interesting to live in a real Hindu house than to stay on board ship. A radio message from Terry's friend, Sir Reginald Forsythe, informed them he would be on hand to greet them and already he and his wife were planning amusements for them. As Terry's friends, they would be welcomed with open arms.

There was not a cloud to mar their proposed visit, although Lois thought it tempting providence for Lenora to keep that scarab she had picked up in Egypt and which had an old Egyptian "curse" inscribed on it.

"Get out the gangplank, Captain!" Lenora shouted to the man at the wheel.

"Oooooo, I almost forgot!" Beverly darted from the deck down the companionway. She reappeared a moment later.

"What's the matter with you?" Lenora demanded.

"The ring Omar El Hamel gave me in New York, remember?" Beverly said, holding up her hand for their inspection. "He said it would bring good fortune and many friends."

"All ashore that's going ashore!" Lois called and dashed for the spot where the two sailors were standing ready to help them ashore.

Sir Reginald Forsythe was indeed on hand to welcome them. He was a jolly, stalwart, sun-tanned officer of the British Army, tall and muscular, with twinkling black eyes and a roguish grin that won all the young people immediately.

Behind Sir Reginald loomed his chief servant, a

lean, chocolate-colored Hindu in a huge white turban which made him look top heavy. He immediately took charge of the baggage.

An automobile was waiting for them and in it they were whisked to the home on the outskirts of the city where their hostess was awaiting them.

During the next few days the young people devoted themselves to sight-seeing and enjoyment. The British air of state and ceremony in Bombay became familiar. The crimson-and-gold liveries of the Viceroy and Governor, the crimson-lined state carriages, the men in scarlet and gold and the splendid horses, all made for the dignity and splendor the Asiatics demanded of their rulers.

Several times they got up at 7 A.M. to ride horseback. They visited the Hindu cave temples of elephants near Bombay. Sir Reginald took it upon himself to be their guide and on one occasion they took a motor trip through the surrounding country. It proved to be a popular idea and they planned a more extended one. They felt that in this way they would see more of the real India.

Early one morning they started out. They went through villages where the natives were busy crushing sugar cane, past sheds where children were being taught, where goats, water buffaloes, and sacred bulls walked leisurely with men, dogs, and women over roads sometimes ankle deep in dust or mud.

The road was shaded with tamarisk and bo trees. They followed the banks of a narrow, muddy river past little hamlets and mud huts. Each group of dwellings had a common well and, under wide-spreading trees, a plastered-up terrace or altar which supported a tiny shrine holding an image of a Hindu god. They went from the Gaya road to a massive white gateway where sheeted Brahmans and turbaned folk stood beside white, noble bullocks and their tilted carts.

A tall, slender Brahman, with the sacred white thread across his shoulder, led the way on a sandy path toward the pinnacle of a temple roof just showing over the tips of the trees. Quite suddenly the scene of all Mahabodhi, or Place of Great Intelligence, was revealed to them.

The sunken courtyard of the Sacred Bo Tree lay at their feet. A nine-storied pyramidal temple rose one hundred and sixty feet into the air. Its gilded pineapple pinnacle seemed almost to brush the clouds.

"In Gautama Buddha's, one of their god's time," Sir Reginald explained for their benefit, "the Bo Tree was sprinkled with milk and perfume and hung with offerings. Buddha taught from his seat beneath the branches. It is a most sacred object and symbol to devout Buddhists—a living replica of Buddha himself."

Sight-seers lingered about the scene, touching the dark-green, heart-shaped leaves of the Bo Tree almost reverently. Beverly was busy securing the right angle of the temple in her camera when she bumped ignominiously into a tall, white-clad figure. Both murmured a polite apology.

Beverly did not look up but continued to adjust her camera. She was taking pictures of all the interesting sights on her trip so she would have tangible evidences of her travels to show the girls at home.

"The temple is too big to get all on one picture," a warm voice said.

It was the man into whom Beverly had bumped, but for a moment she did not recognize the tan face beneath the sun helmet. Only when he took off his hat did she recognize the unruly crop of hair, reckless blue eyes, and engaging grin.

"Larry Owens!" She was dumbfounded.

The young man shook her hand enthusiastically.

"Of all people! The world is a small place after all," he declared with a grin. "Here I was about ready to tear my hair for sight of someone from home and lo and behold I fall over you!"

"I *am* glad to see you!" Beverly declared warmly. "But what are you doing in India? I thought you were somewhere in the western United States on a secret mission for the government. You are certainly hard to keep track of."

Beverly had met Larry Owens for the first time in her sophomore year at Vernon College. Since then their paths had crossed frequently and Larry was one of her most valued friends. But it was the biggest surprise of her life to meet him here so unexpectedly in India.

"I'm on a sort of vacation," Larry said, beaming.

"Beverly, don't you know you shouldn't talk to strange——" Lenora was beginning as she joined her friend. Then her eyes widened in surprise. "Why, it's Larry!"

All the old Alpha girls knew the young man as did the other boys in the party, with the exception of Terry and Sir Reginald. Larry joined their gay group and upon learning that he, as they themselves, was bound for Agra to see the glorious Taj Mahal, their gaiety increased.

The cars they were using were dusty and uncomfortable but they covered the necessary ground. Jests were flung back and forth as the young people proceeded.

"It is a shame your wife and Miss Ernwood didn't come along on this motor trip," Lois declared to Sir Reginald.

"They don't know what they are missing," added Lenora as the car went over a bump and they were jolted severely.

In Agra they found their hotel and some decided to rest for an hour or so, but not Lenora and Beverly. Against strict orders from Sir Reginald and the young men, they started out secretly, alone, to see the native bazaars and congested shopping center.

CHAPTER IV

The Taj Mahal

THE SWINGING LANTERNS of the shops, dim interiors, white-swathed, beturbaned, bearded shopkeepers, dust and chatter did not fail to fascinate both Beverly and Lenora.

"I like this country," Lenora said positively. "Clap your hands and a servant appears. Sir Reginald told me that here in Agra in the hot weather they sometimes put ice in their bathtubs. Imagine, having your own iceberg!"

"Look, Lenora, let's go into this shop. Maybe we can find some things to take home."

Obediently Lenora followed Beverly into a narrow, crowded shop. The Bunia, or shopkeeper, salaamed low before them. Handicapped as they were, not knowing the language, using gestures to interpret their wishes, the girls did very well, but their purchases did not amount to much. They could find nothing to suit them. At last they shook their heads at the shopkeeper and turned toward the door. But he was before them, effectively blocking their entrance, offering numerous articles in his brown hands.

The girls were obdurate. They only wanted to get out of here, but the man was also determined. Now the girls knew why Sir Reginald had cautioned them not to go into the native quarter alone. The natives imposed dreadfully, even threateningly, upon the feminine shoppers.

"Jao!" Beverly exclaimed sharply. It was one word she had learned and it meant "Begone!" but the man still blocked the entrance.

"Miss Gray does not understand you, Mahamet," a suave voice said behind the two girls.

They spun around, but Beverly had already recognized the voice. Count Alexis de Frachiny, or, rather, the man she had known by that name, leaned casually against a pile of oriental rugs.

"My hat!" exclaimed Lenora. "How did you get here?"

"When my plane deposited me in Bombay I did not linger," he said, smiling. "I was almost certain you would come to Agra. All visitors sooner or later come to the Taj Mahal."

"Well?" Beverly interrupted. "Are you still haunting me?" she added humorously.

"Exactly," he bowed again. "I shall continue, as the villains say, to darken your footsteps until I secure what I am after."

"It is too bad your search was interrupted on board our yacht," Beverly said easily.

"Isn't it?" he agreed. "It would have saved me so much time and you so much inconvenience."

"Let's be going, Bev," Lenora said.

"Is your friend going to let us go on our way?" Beverly asked the Count.

The latter spoke briefly to the shopkeeper in his native tongue. Then he turned to the girls.

"I regret very much, but Mahamet seems determined that you shall stay awhile."

Beverly turned and surveyed the Hindu in the doorway. As she did so she pulled her hatbrim a little lower over her forehead. A faint, stray beam of sunlight danced momentarily on the ring on her finger —the ring Omar El Hamel had given her so many months ago in New York when he predicted she would one day visit his country. The shopkeeper stared at the ring, then at Beverly and, past her, at the Count. With a deep salaam he stood aside. The doorway was clear for them.

"Mahamet!" Count Alexis exclaimed sharply.

The girls were surprised. Evidently the tirade of native tongue which the Count poured forth upon the head of the shopkeeper meant nothing to the Hindu. He bowed to the girls and shrugged his shoulders at the Count.

Taking advantage of the abrupt change in the circumstances the girls gained the street in record time and turned toward their hotel.

"What do you suppose made Mahamet change his mind?" Beverly murmured in wonderment.

"I saw him looking at your ring," Lenora said. "It must be a charm or something."

"It certainly was an 'Open sesame' for us," Beverly declared. "I wonder what would have happened——"

"I hope the others are ready to go out to the Taj Mahal," Lenora said dreamily. "It scarcely seems possible that we are here."

She repeated those sentiments when the whole group passed through the sandstone gateway into the outer court with its cabs and bullock carts and peddlers and guides.

The Great Gateway was a magnificent sandstone tower-arch inlaid with white verses and flowers, a tiny row of little bell cupolas bordering the roof line. They could look through the arch to the white dome of the Taj above the cypress trees. Serene, ageless, a miracle of loveliness, the Taj Mahal lived now as it had lived more than two hundred years ago when Shah-Jahan had it built to immortalize his favorite wife, Arjemand. No other woman was ever worshiped in such an exquisite, deathless way.

Lois, her artist's heart thrilled beyond words, lingered longest viewing the setting of white marble against the indigo sky.

They followed the guide into the softly lighted, dim, white interior. A delicate trellis of rare marble workmanship screened the two tombs of Shah-Jahan and his wife. The scrolls and petals of the flowers were of precious stones.

They had seen innumerable lovely and rare sights, historic scenes, fun and danger, but nothing to go deep into their hearts such as this magnificent building built by a man's love and adoration. They felt this sight alone was worth the long trip from New York.

Countless pictures were snapped, each one posing at a different angle to be able to send his photo back to the States with the note "When I saw the Taj Mahal——"

Time flew past and soon they took reluctant farewell of the rarest sight they had yet seen. They went back to their hotel and after a late dinner retired, for they were weary and meant to get an early start on their return journey to Bombay on the morrow.

Beverly lay beside Shirley hopelessly courting sleep. Sleep! It seemed such a waste of time to her. To sleep when they were here within sight and sound of one of the miracles of the world! Well, the others could sleep but she couldn't!

The Taj Mahal had always been something remote, of breathless beauty, something from a fairy story of her childhood. It had been a dream castle, a thing of delicate, exquisite loveliness. Something about which to think and dream. Now it would be ten times more lovely in the moonlight than it had been this afternoon.

Beverly dressed silently in the darkness and when

she stole from the room Shirley still slumbered peacefully. Beverly had donned a light coat, for the nights were cool, but she wore no hat, and the breeze ruffled her curls as she made her way toward the Taj Mahal. She knew guards were placed at the gates at night and no one was allowed in. She wondered just why she had come foolishly all this way to be turned aside. But, she reminded herself, she wasn't to be turned aside! She wanted the actual sight, sound, and touch of the Taj! She was incurably romantic about such things. To her the material achievement of the Taj meant far less than the thought that had erected it. The platform of marble twenty feet high and three hundred feet square, even the dome over the center, more than two hundred feet high, did not mean as much to her as the immortal love Shah-Jahan had had for his beloved Arjemand, "Light of the Palace," when he erected it. She remembered the cruel story of how the Shah, when the Taj was completed, had had the eyes of the artist who conceived it put out so he might never design another like it. Even that seemed to matter little now. The Taj was a thing of reverent beauty, fascinating, awe-inspiring.

She came to the gate they had entered that afternoon. It was closed and a guard leaned nonchalantly against the wall. Beverly went closer. He did not move, except for a perceptible nod of his head. The man was asleep! What luck! On tiptoe Beverly went closer, until she could slide past the guard and through a narrow opening between the gates, into the garden. It did not take her long to lose herself in the shadows of trees and shrubs. And there was the Taj! Like a frost palace in the brilliant light of the stars and moon! The tinkle of running water came to her, mingled in her imagination with the scent of violets and mignonette.

She stood bareheaded in the moonlight and feasted her eyes on the white marble of the tomb. The Taj was not something to see and go away and forget. It was something to see and to feel. The wind was not felt here beneath the stately cypresses. The deserted gardens and lily pools were hushed in starlight. The Taj Mahal was an ivory palace as majestic, as graceful, and as radiant as Arjemand herself must have been. Beverly could almost fancy the lady of the Taj stepping forth from her palace into the moonbeams.

Beverly sat upon a marble bench beside the deepest lily pool and watched and dreamed as the moon mounted higher into the sky. An owl hooted somewhere, dismally. The water in the alabaster pool was deep and clear and the stars overhead were mirrored there. As Beverly leaned over she could see herself pictured in it.

Tonight she dreamed by the Taj Mahal. Only a year ago she was in New York struggling to achieve a measure of fame with her writing, laboring for Charlie Blaine on the staff of the *Tribune*, and probably next year she would again be in New York working. But the Taj Mahal would remain peacefully at rest beneath the indigo sky, changeless as the flow of years. There may have been greater men and lovelier women, but none could be immortalized as Arjemand had been.

A ripple disturbed the surface of the lily pond and Beverly stifled a cry. Beside her reflection had appeared another face. Suddenly from nowhere at all had come another person.

"Shshshshsh," Larry Owens warned laughingly. "You will disturb the ghosts. Don't you know Arjemand and Shah-Jahan are supposed to walk in the garden on lovely nights such as this?"

"I wouldn't blame them. It is too lovely to miss," Beverly said. "But where did you come from?"

"I had to see a man in the village and thought I would come out to see the Taj before I go back to Bombay tomorrow."

"Isn't it strange," Beverly said as he sat down beside her, "that out of all the people in the world we should meet you in India."

"What's so strange about it?" he demanded gaily. "I've always wanted to travel."

"Are you really on a vacation?" she wanted to know.

"Well—sort of," he said.

"Are you on business for the government?" she asked in a thrilled whisper. "What could the States have to do with things over here?"

"Oh, there's an American trying to start trouble over here," he said slowly. "Selling guns to the natives to start an uprising and all that. If anything develops we would be in the middle of the fireworks. I'm looking for him, but the trouble is, or maybe it's a good point, he never stays in one place long. It gives me a chance to see the country."

"We are thinking of going on to Delhi and then farther inland tomorrow instead of going back to Bombay," Beverly said. "Why don't you come with us?"

"I've an engagement I must keep in Bombay," he answered. "You'll see a lot of interesting things in India. I think it is the most mysterious and fascinating country in the world."

"Right now there doesn't seem to be anything but peace and loveliness in the world," Beverly said with a sigh. "The Taj Mahal is so snowy white against the blue sky it is like a dream palace."

"Do you realize it is only one hour before dawn?" he said, smiling. "Have you been here all night?"

"Almost," she laughed. "I suppose we should go before the guards wake up but it is awfully hard to leave. I shall always remember the Taj just as it is now—in the moonlight—lovely and close and friendly."

"Oh, oh!" Larry exclaimed as they turned and went toward the gate. "Here comes trouble."

Watchmen making an early morning round of the garden were approaching them in amazement. Wild gestures, guttural exclamations, painful, misunderstood explanations on Larry's part, ended by both

Beverly and Larry being seized by the outraged dignitaries.

"They probably think we have half the Taj in our pockets," Larry said mournfully.

"Do you suppose we'll go to jail?" Beverly asked laughingly.

"It's serious," he growled. "I don't know what the beggars will do. I wish I could speak Hindustani."

Beverly suddenly had an idea. She slipped the ring Omar El Hamel had given her off her finger and gave it to Larry.

"Show them this," she said.

"What good will it do?" he wanted to know.

"I'm not sure," she answered. "Try it anyhow."

Larry halted in his pace and refused to budge when the guard pulled at his arm. In the light from one of the lanterns Larry called the man's attention to the ring. Instantly the man was alert. Beverly's captor released his hold on her arm. The men stood at attention, respectful once more. One talked fluently, his gestures apologetic, and they both escorted Beverly and Larry to the gateway, bowing as the Americans took a hasty exit.

"What is it, a charm?" Larry demanded as he handed Beverly back her ring. "It certainly made those fellows sit up and take notice. Perhaps they thought we were Shah-Jahan and Arjemand come back to life."

"That is the second time the ring has come to my rescue," Beverly said. "I'm glad I've got it."

For the second time in twenty-four hours Beverly's ring proved to be a valuable aid. In both cases it had let her escape unscathed from circumstances which might have been serious. Yet, unknown to her, the hardest trial was yet to come, a trial which would prove the infallibility of Omar's gift.

CHAPTER V

The Boat Wreck

"'FROM Greenland's icy mountains, From India's Coral Strand——'" quoted Lenora, with gestures, as the two cars sped over the route from Agra to Delhi.

"She has started again," Lois said sadly to Terry. "Can't you do anything about it?"

Terry grinned consolingly. "Perhaps she has forgotten the rest of it. We will hope so anyway."

"I have not," Lenora said, making an impish face at him. She proceeded to recite fluently what she had started.

The others in the car, Lois, Terry, Paul, and Miss Ernwood, had to bear up courageously. Beverly, Jim, Shirley, and Roger were in the first car with Sir Reginald.

The group had left their hotel early in the morning and were now almost at their destination. Larry had hastily bidden them farewell, claiming receipt of a telegram which called him back immediately to Bombay. However, they made arrangements to meet again, if possible, in Singapore.

It had been hard for Beverly to rise jubilantly and as fresh as the rest when she had had only an hour of sleep. But the excitement of new scenes and continued action buoyed her to keen enjoyment.

Sir Reginald recounted various experiences of his in India and kept his guests well amused and entertained as the cars proceeded. The young people shouted back and forth to one another until the inhabitants of the villages they passed must have wondered about such strange visitors.

At Delhi, during their brief stop there, the young people were interested visitors to the famous Peacock Throne in the Audience Hall at the Fort. The tail of the glorified bird shimmered in the natural colors of rubies, diamonds, sapphires, and emeralds valued at thirty-five million dollars.

They passed a garden where a man, whom the people regarded as a saint, sat in the sun.

"What's so wonderful about him?" Lenora wanted to know.

"He hasn't spoken in twenty-three years," Sir Reginald answered.

"There is an example for you to follow, Lenora," Lois giggled.

"You will find a lot of such people in India," Sir Reginald continued. "People who, in order to insure their safe passage to heaven, impose penitence on themselves. In some parts of India people worship snakes. In Nepal there are the monkey worshipers, religious fanatics who worship the beasts in temples, and woe to the white man who touches a monkey there. The men themselves remind me of monkeys, bearded faces, beady eyes, filthy——"

"I hope we aren't going to Nepal," Lois said brightly.

Sir Reginald laughed. "No. Tonight and tomorrow we shall spend at Lahore in the house of the Lieutenant Governor of Punjab. Then the next day we shall go on to a small community composed almost entirely of British officers and their wives where you girls can stay in my old bungalow while we men go hunting tigers and elephants."

"I want to go hunting, too," Lenora said.

Terry laughed. "This is one time you will have to stay behind."

Lenora saw the force of his argument.

"All right," she said airily. "I dare say we can find something to do while you are gone."

Terry didn't like that. Even in his short acquaintance with her he had come to know that Lenora seeking excitement usually found what she went after. He contented himself with a heavy frown in her direction. Words of caution would mean nothing to her, so he wisely kept still.

"Lahore," Sir Reginald informed the young people riding in his car, once they had started again, "was here before Alexander the Great came. It is surrounded by the remains of the old city wall. It is, also, where Kipling began his work in a local newspaper office."

They found a warm welcome awaiting them at Lahore. Everywhere they went they found cordiality and friendliness.

Their day in Lahore provided a big thrill. The Lieutenant Governor bestowed upon Beverly and Lenora the coveted honor of riding on his parade elephant.

"My Lord the Elephant," a bell hanging from his neck, his trunk swinging from side to side, his bulk shuffled along on his cushioned feet, made his own way on the narrow street. From the howdah on his back the girls could see all the domestic life in the quarter, from the squatting merchant on his doorsill, broad avenues of British residential quarters and government houses, to the English and Catholic cathedrals and fine buildings of Aitchison College.

"This is fine for a bird's-eye view," Lenora said, "but I'm getting seasick." The girls were swayed from side to side with each step of the big beast.

"It isn't any worse than riding the camel we did in Cairo," Beverly said.

Lenora looked over the side. "It is, too," she maintained. "We're farther from the ground."

In the afternoon they went out to the polo ground. White and brown, English and Indians, played together. The Indian players were light and supple, depending upon their wrists and resiliency of the shafts of their mallets to send the ball over the hard ground.

"This is more exciting than a football game," Lenora cried, eyes shining, breathless with excitement, hopping up and down beside Terry as the Englishmen drove home a goal.

Altogether their brief stay in Lahore was memorable. The next day they left to drive even farther into northern India.

They found the bungalow to which Sir Reginald took them a rambling, comfortable affair in the best approved Hindu style. Silent-footed servants supplied their every need. The building was within sound of the native city, yet outside. The British cantonment was almost a mile away. Here, too, there was a polo field and race course to provide amusement and excitement for the residents and any visitors.

The bungalow was surrounded on three sides by a dense mass of jungle grass. The grass stretched away into a forest, farther on, where the young men looked forward eagerly to a lengthy hunt for wild pigs and tigers.

One morning the five men, with Sir Reginald as instructor and guide, started out with native gunbearers. The girls were content to remain comfortably in the bungalow.

"However," Lenora said positively, "I expect you to bring me back a nice tiger rug!"

"Or an elephant—no less!" added Lois with a laugh.

The girls spent the day writing letters, catching up on lost sleep, reading magazines, or taking pictures.

Needless to say, this inactivity could not last another day.

Early in the morning Lenora was up, demanding something to do. They did not expect the young men back until the following day, so there were many hours to be filled somehow.

"Achmed," she demanded of Sir Reginald's chief of staff, who could speak excellent English, "what can we do today?"

"What is the Mem-sahib's pleasure?"

"We don't know," put in Lois. "What do the Englishmen living here do?"

"Mem-sahib, there is a race today. Excellent riders, huge crowds."

At that the girls smiled. Huge crowds! The whole community wouldn't make a huge crowd, but they did not argue the point.

"I don't feel like a race," Beverly put in. "How about a boat on the river. Is there a boat we could ride on a short trip?"

"Mem-sahib, there is a boat crossing the river with cattle, but nothing pleasing for the Mem-sahibs."

"I think I'll go to the race," Shirley said.

"I will go with you," Miss Ernwood decided laughingly. "A cattle boat has no appeal for me."

"Beverly and I are more stout-hearted, aren't we, Bev? We'll go for a boat ride—even if we have to sit with the cows," Lenora decided.

Achmed bowed deferentially. "Sir Reginald would not advise the cattle boat, Mem-sahib."

"It doesn't make any difference," Lenora said. "We'll go. It will be an experience to write home to Connie and Kathleen about."

Lois giggled. "They would probably say we were in our native environment at last."

"Where does the boat leave, Achmed?" Beverly asked.

"But a little way down the road is a path which leads to the river front. It is there. But, Mem-sahib —it is not fitting that the young ladies should go."

"Do you really think we shouldn't?" Lois wondered.

"Perhaps we had better give it up," Beverly said. "It might not be just the thing for us——"

"Nonsense!" Lenora said heartily. "Since when did we always do the proper thing? We're out for fun, excitement, atmosphere, or what they have here. I say we go!"

"You will go, too, Achmed," Beverly said. "Please let us know what time."

"Soon after luncheon, Mem-sahib," Achmed said with a bow and went away. He did not approve, but there was nothing more he could do. It was not his responsibility if the foolish Americans desired to expose themselves to needless dangers.

The boat proved to be what Achmed had said— totally unfitting. Dirt, filth, mooing cows, sacred white oxen, and a mixture of humanity such as the girls had never seen were crowded on a small, flat, barge-like affair.

The girls, with Achmed, brown and tall and serious in the background, found a place at the rail as the boat put off from shore.

"At least we can breathe here at the rail," Lois said thankfully.

Only three of them had come; Shirley and Miss Ernwood, laughingly, selected the race to attend in place of this river jaunt. Now the other three secretly wished themselves with their two friends. It would be much more pleasant than this hot, close mass of humanity—animals and humans.

"Major Kilgore!" Beverly said delightedly as a tall, military man made his way to them.

"What are you doing on this frightful craft?" the Englishman, to whom Sir Reginald had introduced them before he went off on the hunting trip, demanded, wiping his red, perspiring face with an already damp handkerchief.

"Getting acquainted with the real India," Lenora said gaily. "Beverly is a writer and we are hunting atmosphere for her."

They were glad of the added prestige and support the Englishman gave them.

The river water was dirty and muddy and the craft labored slowly through it.

"He's carrying a heavy load this trip," Major Kilgore declared. "Hope he makes it to the shore."

"So do I!" Lenora said fervently. "I've no desire to take a bath in this water!"

"The Ganges is a holy river," Lois reminded her.

"It purges one of his sins. The Hindus bathe in it and drink it."

"For me—no, thanks!" Lenora said.

"Major, will you take me down into the hold?" Beverly asked. "As long as I am here I want to see everything."

The Major and Beverly made their way through the crowd. They had a brief glimpse into the hold where restless, ill-at-ease cattle stamped about.

"If they all decided to trot to one side of the boat at the same time the craft would upset, wouldn't it?" Beverly asked.

"Right you are!" the Major agreed. "We will hope they don't."

Going back up to the upper deck into the fresh air was a difficult task. The Major went first, making way for Beverly.

The girl, endeavoring to keep close to him, felt, suddenly, a grasp upon her wrist. A second later she was released—minus her wrist watch. Now, the watch was Beverly's most prized possession, presented to her by the girls of Vernon College for heroism. She did not now intend to lose it. She had a glimpse of a brown smiling face. A native woman, dirty, ragged, and unkempt, turned away, the watch shining for a moment in her hand. Beverly turned to shout to the Major. He was already a good distance away. Surely she could handle the native!

Beverly turned back, seeking the woman. The native was already going down into the hold. Beverly did not relish another trip into that hot, dirty place but her watch was valuable! After a brief moment's hesitation she followed quickly.

"Where's Beverly?" Lenora asked of the Major.

"Right here—— I say! She was right behind me a moment ago," he said.

"She'll turn up," Lois said confidently.

"I'll go after her. I——" A ludicrous look of surprise appeared on the Major's face as the boat swayed under their feet.

Glances were exchanged. Voices began an excited jabbering. In the hold cattle reared their heads and snorted viciously. Simultaneously they rushed against the men who had brought them on board. With the weight shifting from an even distribution to one side, the frail river craft wavered. One side settled lower and lower until, unable to hold its equilibrium, it capsized, sending natives, Americans, cattle, men, and women into the brown water.

CHAPTER VI

Lost

PANIC surged through the struggling mass in the water. No one who survived would ever forget the terror, dismay, and horror of the scene.

The river was too wide and the boat had progressed too far out into the stream for those who could to swim back to their starting place. Instead, terrified men and women clung to the overturned craft which was even now settling lower and lower into the water. Some, such as the two American girls, struck out determinedly for the opposite shore scarcely more than two hundred yards away. To stay at the spot was dangerous, for striving, trapped humans and animals were struggling wildly and when the boat finally sank below the surface it would suck strugglers into the whirlpool—down to destruction.

It was the longest, most difficult task either of the girls had ever had to do—gain the shore. When finally they succeeded they were completely spent.

"Lenora——" Lois called, struggling upright.

"Right here," Lenora said, not stirring from her position prone on the ground.

About them other survivors sought the dry land. The scene in the water was ghastly. The air was rent with cries.

"Where's Beverly?" Lois wanted to know anxiously.

"I haven't seen her," Lenora said.

"There's the Major!" Lois cried.

The splendor of Major Kilgore's uniform was sadly ruined, but he greeted the girls thankfully.

"Where's Beverly?" Lois demanded. "Did you find her?"

The Major shook his head.

"No. I couldn't reach her in time."

"Bev's a good swimmer," Lenora said bravely. "She'll make the shore all right."

"It's every man for himself out there," Lois said with a glance at the struggle still going on in the water. "Look!"

The barge settled farther and farther into the water until it was lost from sight. The suction created by the sinking boat made a whirlpool into which were dragged the frantic survivors who had not fled the scene soon enough.

Lois turned her back. The horror would invade her sleeping and waking hours with vivid reality. For days and nights to come she would hear the screams and cries of trapped humans and animals.

The shore was soon crowded with those who had

managed to gain its banks. But, though they searched diligently among the crowds, the two Americans and the British officer could find no trace of Beverly. It was as though she had been swallowed in the whirl-pool!

Hours passed, hours filled with dread and anxiety and work to help those who had been injured by the wreckage or panic-stricken mob. Finally another boat arrived on the scene and transported them back to the landing stage from which the barge had left.

The girls gained the bungalow and found Achmed, worn from his own struggles, seeking them. But he, too, had not a trace of Beverly. It had been a forlorn hope that she would somehow have gained the shore and be waiting for them at the bungalow.

Shirley and Miss Ernwood, totally unaware of the afternoon's happenings, arrived warm and excited and happy from the races.

Lenora and Lois had changed from their water-soaked clothes and were busy pacing the veranda. Their worried frame of mind was discernible from their faces.

"What's the matter with you two?" Shirley demanded dropping into a long wicker chair. "The races were grand. Such riding! How was the boat ride? Aren't you back early?"

"It's the first time I ever walked home from a boat ride," Lenora said, running nervous fingers through her hair.

"We had a bath in the river," added Lois.

Shirley laughed. "For goodness sake, what happened?"

Lenora, her story-telling ability at its height, told Shirley and Miss Ernwood about the tragedy.

"There must have been many lives lost," she ended slowly.

"Maybe Beverly was one of them," Lois burst out.

"What?" Shirley was on her feet, gripping Lois' arm tensely. "What do you mean?"

"I mean, we haven't been able to find Beverly since," Lois said.

"You mean, she might have——"

"Stop it!" Lenora said passionately. "Cheerful cherubs, you are! Why do you always have to believe the worst? Beverly's had a charmed life so far—let's hope it hasn't failed her now."

"We've got to look at things as they are," Lois insisted stubbornly. "Beverly was going back below deck—at least, she wasn't with the Major or us on the upper deck. I doubt if any of those caught below deck had a chance when the boat went over."

"What are we sitting here doing nothing for?" Shirley demanded.

"Major Kilgore has promised to start an investigation," Lois said. "Achmed, too, has gone out to see what he can find."

As the hours passed their anxiety mounted. The Major could report nothing encouraging when he dropped in at dinnertime that evening. Achmed returned also empty-handed.

Dinner was a sorry affair. The girls had no appe-tite; even Lenora's determinedly cheery outlook failed. Beverly's absence set a cloud of gloom over their heads. They could not explain the silence that surrounded the disappearance of their chum—unless she had really gone down into the muddy depths of the river with the boat. Of that they tried not to think. On the other hand, if she had succeeded in re-maining afloat and finally reached the shore she should have been able to reach the bungalow by this time.

After dinner they went into the living room and stared gloomily at one another.

Suddenly outside arose a clatter and chorus of voices. The young men were returning hours ahead of time. The girls had never been so glad to see them as they were now. At last there would be action!

"Look what we've got!" Paul called gaily, indicat-ing the huge striped tiger skin two of the servants produced.

"A friend of yours, Lenora," Terry said mis-chievously, "refused to let me come back without him."

A tiny, furry monkey jumped from Terry's shoul-der into Lenora's arms.

At any other time Lenora would have been de-lighted. Now the monkey produced only a grin and a faint response.

"Who's sick?" Roger wanted to know. "You all look about as cheerful as caged alligators."

"We're about as helpless, too," Lois put in.

Jim threw his hat at a chair. It hooked expertly on the arm.

"Where's Beverly?" he asked.

"That's it in a nutshell," Shirley said.

"That's what?" Sir Reginald demanded.

"Will you please stop talking in riddles?" Roger added. "What's wrong with you?"

"We're scared and worried and——"

"But why?" Terry asked.

For the second time Lenora told the story of the boat and their subsequent plunge into the river. Major Kilgore assured the concerned and surprised new arrivals that everything was being done. He had soldiers from the British cantonment searching along the river. Achmed had enlisted the aid of some of his fellow countrymen and questions were being asked among all the survivors.

"But is that all we can do?" Jim demanded irately.

"It seems dreadful to sit here doing nothing," Shirley agreed, pacing up and down.

It seemed that waiting was about all any of them could do. It would do no good for them to go and search along the river front. Strangers in the country as they were, it might mean they would be lost and so cause more harm than good.

Major Kilgore made the bungalow his temporary headquarters and all reports of the search were made to him there.

It grew late. The jungle night settled down. Now

and then they could hear an owl hoot dismally. There was no use to think of retiring. Each knew he would not sleep. Shirley and Lois sat on the veranda. Lenora and Miss Ernwood remained with the Major and the others talking.

Suddenly through the gateway of the yard came Achmed, his movement noiseless in his bare feet, but the man he was dragging behind him was howling uproariously.

The pandemonium brought the others tumbling out posthaste.

"Achmed! What is it?" Sir Reginald demanded.

Achmed thrust the prostrate Hindu upon the veranda and kicked him distastefully with his foot.

"Sahib," he bowed to Sir Reginald, "I have been among my people and those saved from the boat. As the Sahib knows, I, too, have been seeking the American Mem-sahib."

"Does this man know anything?" Sir Reginald asked tensely.

"If he does make him speak!" the Major put in loudly.

"He has already spoken but not enough, Sahib," Achmed bowed.

"Well?" The young people crowded closer.

From the wide girdle about his waist Achmed drew a small, shiny article and held it up in the light streaming from the open doorway of the bungalow. It glowed in the yellow lamplight. Each one there recognized it. Achmed had Beverly's wrist watch!

"Achmed!" Shirley snatched the watch from the Hindu's grasp. "Where did you get this?"

"From this son of an evil father!" Achmed said, prodding the native on the floor.

"Where did he get it?" Jim wanted to know, his face dark and strained.

Achmed spoke rapidly in a guttural voice to the man on the floor. When he stood up and faced the others his eyes were tiny pin points of light, his face an inscrutable mask.

"Sahib, he says he—seeking evilly for his own good——"

"Where? Where?" Lenora cried.

"From a drowning woman," Achmed said.

"What?" The word shot from the Major like a report from a gun. The others were speechless.

Sir Reginald and Jim moved at the same time but the younger man was closest to the native. Jim dragged the native to his feet and held the man against the wall, a hand at his throat.

"Ask him, Achmed, where this was."

Achmed moved closer. Words flowed sharply from his lips. The native cowered, but he talked in response.

"Sahibs," Achmed turned about and permitted himself the briefest of smiles, "it was an ayah—a servant—not the American Mem-sahib."

Lenora emitted a long-drawn-out sigh. Shirley sank weakly into a chair. She felt that her knees would not support her. Relief overpowered them all.

"He got the wrist watch from a native woman," Lois said slowly. "But where did she get it?"

"That he does not know," Achmed said.

"Beverly never parted with it—willingly!" Lenora interposed.

"Shall I take charge of this man?" the Major asked Sir Reginald.

Sir Reginald nodded. "See if you or anyone can get any more information out of him."

"I will go again, Sahib, to the river," Achmed said.

"You have done well, Achmed," Sir Reginald called as the chief of his servants melted into the thick shadows about the veranda.

The girls took Beverly's watch inside. On the table among the magazines it lay and sparkled up at them.

"I wish I was a magician," Lenora said, "and could make that watch talk."

Glowingly warm in the lamplight the little watch lay before them. In its tiny case it held the secret of Beverly's whereabouts—at least, so they thought. Their anxiety could be allayed, the mystery of Beverly's disappearance solved, if the tiny watch had the power of speech.

CHAPTER VII

Rescue

Upon leaving the Major, Beverly turned and made her way to the rickety stairs that led below deck. Momentarily she lost sight of the native woman she was following. It was while she paused on the steps, scanning the scene below, that the disaster occurred.

The ship, if such it could be called, lurched sideways. Beverly caught frantically at the rafters overhead to steady herself. People were thrown to the floor. Water poured down the open stairs and in through the porthole. There was a concerted rush for the upper deck. Beverly was caught in a crushing, struggling mass of natives. She was carried along helplessly, unable to free herself. The terror-stricken natives fought desperately for their lives.

There was no chance of rejoining her friends; she could not even find them. The craft was in an uproar. The boat settled lower and lower, finally capsizing and, when it did, Beverly, like the others, was thrown into the water, but she had been in such a tight mass of humans she had more of a struggle to come to the surface unhindered.

Brown hands clutched at her and brown arms dragged her under. Water gurgled in her ears and blurred her vision. And now Beverly was fighting like the rest for air and freedom and life. She was fully aware of the danger presented by the sinking vessel and knew she must get away from it as quickly as possible. Coming to the surface, she started out for the nearest shore line. But the water was full of figures. Pitiful sights tugged at her heart. Stopping to help this person, to hold that one up, Beverly was caught off guard when the barge sank. The whirlpool caught her, whipping her about. She was flung against something hard and hung onto it grimly.

Beverly felt as if she had swallowed half the river when she was free of the whirlpool. Her limbs were heavy, refusing to obey the urgency she put upon them. She recognized the fact that she was dangerously near to sinking not to rise again. But she wouldn't give up! Blindly she fought to remain afloat. The water was sweeping her away from the scene of the tragedy, downstream. She thought fleetingly of Lois and Lenora, wondering if they were safe. If only she could find them! But she knew she had very little strength left.

At last, spent and bruised, Beverly was hurled helplessly onto the shore—far from the spot her two friends had gained. She was too exhausted to move and lay on the good, solid earth, grateful for the sun's warmth on her back. She did not know how long she lay there but soon it began to get cooler. She stood up and looked around. The sun was going down rapidly and the evening air was becoming cooler. Not a living thing stirred as far as she could see. The water lapped against the shore at her feet. Behind her in the forest she could hear the faint chattering of monkeys. Suddenly a giant crow waddled into sight. Gray doves circled overhead.

Beverly frowned thoughtfully. What should she do now? She certainly couldn't swim across the river. She shivered at the mere thought. She had no desire to see water again for months. Would she ever forget the terror of those terrible minutes in the water? But her immediate predicament was more important at the moment than thinking of what had happened. She contemplated the forest at her back. The dark depths did not appeal to her. She visualized snakes, even tigers, deep in the jungle.

Yet to remain aimlessly where she was did not help. She must get back to the bungalow. The girls, if they were safe, would be worried. If they were safe! She fervently hoped they were.

A narrow footpath led from the shore into the dense jungle growth and this, after due deliberation, she followed. She was growing colder by the minute and she was hungry and tired, but she must find some sort of shelter or civilization before she could hope for any measure of comfort.

Progress was slow and laborious. She went cautiously, not knowing at what moment she might find an animal or snake confronting her. Night was coming on like a heavy blanket now. In a little while it would be completely dark. At the thought of the black jungle night Beverly shivered. If only she had a flashlight and something with which to defend herself!

Her nerves were on edge from her experiences of the day and every sound was magnified tenfold. The cry of a jackal made her stop still, trembling. A flying fox or grouse stirred the bushes. Every moment she expected to step on a deadly cobra or rattlesnake.

The path wound round and round between the trees and dense jungle grass. It seemed endless. Beverly began to wish she had stayed back along the shore of the river. As it was, suppose she came to a pool which was inhabited by crocodiles and alligators and to which wild elephants and other jungle animals came at night to drink?

"Steady!" she warned herself. Mustn't let imagination run away with her!

She went on steadily, hoping against hope to see some signs of civilization.

Night was upon the jungle now and even the brilliant moon did not penetrate through the tree branches over Beverly's head. She was completely alone in the dark, mysterious world of nature.

Moments seemed ages to the girl. The night would be a thousand years long at this rate. She thought of the warm bungalow, a delicious dinner, and a comfortable bed. What she wouldn't give for them right now! Had she wanted new and exciting adventures? Had she ever wanted to explore the hidden and mysterious depths of innermost India? It was what she was doing but she did not find it as glamorous as she had once imagined it.

A pair of green eyes shone from the darkness on her right. She fled the spot in panic. She heard the beating of wings overhead, cries of night prowlers, and, more menacing, the pad-pad of heavy feet on the path behind her. A terrified glance showed those same fiery eyes approaching nearer and nearer. A low growl issued from the darkness.

Blind, unreasoning terror took possession of Beverly. She fled wildly, aimlessly following the path, now and then stumbling over twigs or holes in the ground. She did not know what new terror this was on her heels but she wanted to leave it as far behind as possible.

Was that a point of light up ahead? Inspired anew by the hope of rescue, she ran more swiftly, recklessly. She could smell the smoke of a campfire and as she came nearer she could see the glimmer of tents in the flickering light.

Nearer and nearer came that menace on the path behind her. She could hear the heavy breathing of the animal and she did not dare turn round to see what manner of creature it was. She sped on toward that friendly campfire. Even if it proved to be no more than a group of native hunters they would be more comforting than a lone journey in the jungle with a tiger apt to spring upon her at any minute.

Frightened, totally unable to calm herself, Beverly flung herself forward into the circle of firelight, stumbled, fell, and lay still, unknowing and past caring that the tiger chose that moment to spring upon his prey.

A rifle cracked. A spurt of flame flashed. The tiger faltered, pawed the air wildly, and collapsed beside the girl. Natives came running. The white man with the rifle came closer. While the natives awfully stared at the tiger he carried the girl into his tent.

Beverly found her good Samaritan to be a ruddy, stalwart, brother American, with a flashing smile, friendly eyes, and a delightful sense of humor.

"And now will you please tell me how you came to be running about the jungle without so much as a flashlight?" he demanded finally.

From the depths of the blanket in which she was wrapped while she slowly sipped a bowl of hot broth Beverly told him her story.

"I guess I rather went to pieces at the end," she finished, blushing.

"I should jolly well think you would," he said admiringly.

"Are you a writer?" she asked, nodding toward the typewriter standing on a small table beside sheaves of paper and magazines.

He grinned. "Discovered! I'm an explorer-writer. My work is mostly technical."

"Are you by any chance Anthony Anton who writes for those archaeologic magazines and weekly periodicals?"

He nodded. "I dig up old ruins and write about them." He stood up. "Now you must rest and in the morning we'll take you back to your friends."

CHAPTER VIII

Sight-Seeing

"SOME PEOPLE have all the luck!" Lenora sighed.

"If you call it luck to be lost in a shipwreck and chased by a man-eating tiger, you are more than welcome to my share of it," Beverly laughed.

It was the following morning. Scarcely after dawn Beverly and Anthony Anton had ridden from his camp to a narrow ford through which their sturdy little horses could wade across to the opposite bank of the river. In little more than an hour Beverly and Mr. Anton dismounted before Sir Reginald's bungalow.

To an excited and eager audience and over a breakfast in which Mr. Anton joined them her story was told.

"By the way," Mr. Anton smiled, "I shall have that tiger skinned for you and you may have it for a rug. It is a fine specimen."

The explorer declined their pressing invitation to spend at least the rest of the day with them and shortly before lunch he rode away, waving a gay farewell from astride his horse.

It was as they watched his departure that Lenora had made her remark concerning the fortune of some of her fellow men.

"I mean your luck in being rescued by someone like Anthony Anton. Ah me!" Lenora sighed.

"Now that Beverly is back are we going to move again?" Lois wanted to know, ignoring Lenora.

"Why should we go away when Mr. Anton is in the neighborhood?" Lenora persisted. "Let's stay here awhile."

"I think we should go on as soon as possible," Terry said, with a wicked glance in Lenora's direction. It was common knowledge among the others that the young Englishman had lost his heart to the madcap American girl. Even so, they continued to tease each other unmercifully, for Lenora was evasive about the state of her heart.

"Mr. Anton told me his camp is moving on tomorrow," added Beverly.

"In that case," Lenora shrugged, "we might as well go on."

Accordingly, that very afternoon the young people set out on the last lap of their journey to Peshawar, the valley of Kashmir, and the Khyber Pass. Persisting in their desire to avoid the usual tourist routes and delve deeper into the real India, the young people were keenly interested in the scenes to come.

The Vale of Kashmir was astounding. It would

soon be lush with the fresh green of sprouting rice paddies, of waving poplar trees. Ten miles to each wall of mountains, covered with unbroken snow, and rising as high as twenty-two thousand feet into the clouds.

"Actually the Himalayas!" Beverly whispered, eyes sparkling. She snuggled deeper into her coat for it was cold.

When they came to Srinagar they were surprised at the strange natural beauty. It reminded them of Venice, with its panorama of canals and water crafts. There were almost no streets in this ancient city, but they found the winding waterways charming even in winter. It was easy to imagine its even greater cool green beauty of summer.

They made tours of the art shops which bordered the Jhelum River, buying almost every kind of oddity from oriental rugs to soft and exquisite Kashmir shawls.

On their last night they paid homage to the little paradise of marble, Shalimar. Built by a Mongol emperor for his queen it combined nature's best forces to make one of the most romantic spots in Kashmir.

Before long, however, the Himalayas, towering cold and ice-covered, were luring the young people on.

Though the temperature of Peshawar in winter was usually bitter cold, a freak of nature seemed to travel with the Americans and though they found the country cold it was nothing they had not experienced before. Perhaps it was a hint of spring to come.

They found the streets of the Muhammadan City of Peshawar crowded with fierce-looking men, Kashmiris, Nepalese, Tibetans, all armed.

Arriving Thursday night they dined immediately at the home of the General commanding, amid the splendor of many uniforms and medals on the young subalterns, but retired early to their government-dak bungalow that they might see the convoy trains at dawn the following day.

Two times a week, on Tuesdays and Fridays, caravans go unmolested through the Khyber Pass to and from Afghanistan. Only on those two days of the week is travel safe. On other days one travels at his own risk.

It was then, early in the morning, that hundreds of camels, donkeys, and oxen, loaded with merchandise from Central Asia, Afghanistan, and beyond, shuffled along, noses in the air, beside bellowing drivers.

The young people found it all noise and bustle and dust when the caravan from the south met the caravan from the north. The gurgling of camels loaded with boxes of tea, furniture, pans, and kettles, the shouts of drivers, now and then the yelp of a dog, all made the scene one of general confusion.

Yet it was not only the caravans that impressed them.

"The Khyber Pass!" Beverly murmured. "You

know, one doesn't actually realize what it is until one sees it—feels the air that hangs over it."

"Mmmmm," Lenora agreed. "My encyclopedia described it merely as 'A great pass from India to Afghanistan, thirty-three miles long and ten to four hundred and fifty feet wide.' It left out all the glamour!"

"G-glamour?" Lois questioned with a shiver, for the early morning wind was ice-tinged.

"Think of the romance and the battles fought here," Terry said impressively. "The very air is filled with the ghosts of great armies—Alexander and his Greeks, the Persians, the English—for thirty centuries this pass has been the key to India. Why, through all these years——"

"Terry, do you feel well?" Lenora interrupted sweetly. "Perhaps we had better go back where it is warmer. I don't think the lofty mountain air agrees with Terry," she told the others, a mischievous twinkle in her eyes.

"Was it about this section that Tennyson's 'Charge of the Light Brigade' was written?" someone asked.

"No, that was the Crimea. But anyway—'Cannon to the right of them,'" Terry quoted obligingly, "'Cannon to the left of them, Cannon in front of them——'"

"And Lenora behind them! No wonder they went onward!" dared Lois.

"I could eat another breakfast now," Lenora said brightly, ignoring Lois and her remark.

They turned back, and that very afternoon found them hurrying southward.

"I'll be glad to get back on the yacht," Lenora sighed. "We've covered so much ground and seen so much in such a short space of time I'm getting dizzy."

"You don't want a rest, do you?" Lois asked in surprise.

"Well," Lenora drawled, "of course if I would be missing anything——" she began hastily, and the others laughed.

Their return stay in Bombay was of short duration. They went immediately to the yacht and, bidding a grateful farewell to Sir Reginald, the Americans collected their mail and the "Susabella" sailed away to new ports.

"At least we haven't said good-by to India yet," Lenora said satisfactorily. "We still have to see Ceylon and Calcutta and Benares."

The "Susabella," when it hoisted anchor in the harbor of Bombay, pointed its prow south to sail round the point of India and up the eastern shore line, where the Americans would still have a chance to see the points of interest they had missed.

Lenora looked around at her four traveling companions who still remained on deck. Shirley, Lois, Roger, and Terry were all deeply engrossed in their mail. Lenora supposed that the others, Miss Ernwood, Beverly, Jim, and Paul, were likewise engrossed below the deck in their cabins. Resignedly, Lenora turned to her own sheaf of letters.

It was many weeks since the young people had received word from families and friends in the States, and letters had accumulated invitingly in the mail. Most of them had been forwarded from Cairo, their last stopping place at which they had received mail. The time it took the hotel to send them on to Bombay must have been what caused the delay in the beginning and the reason they did not receive their missives before they went on their tour of India.

Beverly lay on her bunk and leisurely enjoyed each letter before going on to the next. Her parents had written long, newsy letters, then there was one from Virginia Harris, her old college chum who was in medical school, and one from Kathleen Ryan, and, purposely Beverly had saved this one for the last, one from Connie Elwood. In gay conspiracy with Shirley, Connie had been the one to submit Beverly's book anew when the young authoress herself had become sorely discouraged and sick at heart. Always, Beverly would look upon any success she might achieve as a direct result of Connie's confidence in her. If it had not been for Connie, Beverly would not even be on board the "Susabella" now. Instead, she would be back in New York slaving away at her newspaper job. She remembered vividly the pluck and determination she had needed when she made her decision in Paris to go back to New York and forge some measure of success from apparent failure. Then, in the nick of time, had come Connie's cable that her, Beverly's, book had been sold to a firm of publishers.

Along with Connie's letter was a package, securely wrapped. This, Beverly discovered from the letter, was a copy of her own book, just as it had come from the presses weeks before. True to her word, Connie had sent her her copy. Beverly's eyes danced over the closely written pages of her friend's letter and then, with fingers that trembled with eagerness, she opened her first book.

It was a thrill that words could not express. In her hands she held something of her own creation, something that would endure, something she had molded from nothing at all. A sense of achievement swelled her heart with pride. The months of striving, discouragement, and tears were as naught. They did not matter now. Only the fact that at last she had given something to the world. No one could ever take away from her the pride in her first accomplishment. The book was a part of her and for years it would live on. People, unknown and untold, would read it, and through the printed page she would draw a little closer to them.

The artist's conception for the cover and frontispiece were original and intriguing. Connie had written that it was already exceedingly popular. That was an added source of satisfaction. Achievement, accomplished work, always meant more when one's work was appreciated.

The quotation "I know happiness for I have done good work" came to her mind and she agreed heartily with it. She was immensely happy at that moment.

Bits of her own gallant spirit and philosophy of life were tangible things now.

Up on deck Lenora was perusing newspaper clippings with a wide grin.

"Listen to this," she told the others. "Kathleen sent them to me. They're bits of literary critics' columns —commenting on Bev's book. The *Tribune* takes a fatherly pride in its cherub," she said gleefully. "They say it is 'surprising that one as young and charming as the authoress should have such a wide acquaintance with life and its different moods.' "

"That's something," Lois grinned.

"Here's one that says 'the authoress is indubitably slated for a huge success in the world's elite literary circles.' " Lenora winked. "Another says it is 'the most entertaining and gripping story of recent months.' "

"First thing we know, Beverly will be famous," Shirley smiled. "I'm glad her book is becoming popular. It would have broken her heart if it hadn't."

"Let's go down and congratulate our young authoress," Lenora proposed, hopping up.

Lenora opened the door to Beverly's cabin and winked over her shoulder at the others.

"Look at the conceited thing! Reading her own book—as if she didn't know every word in it by heart!"

"Let's see it, Bev," Shirley cried. "I wish Connie had sent me one!"

There were more exclamations, ohs and ahs, over

Beverly's book. Only now was it really borne in upon them that this member of their jolly party had real talent. They were just beginning to realize what a task Beverly had set for herself. It had been the same with Shirley's stage career. Only when that young lady had distinguished herself before the world had the others realized that under the gay comradeship lay ability and ambition and talent.

In due course of time the rest of the party were shown Beverly's literary masterpiece and dinner was made a festive occasion in honor of their distinguished member.

After dinner they spent hours discussing the adventures they had had in India and were still to have.

Day by day, hour by hour, they drew nearer to China. China, the mysterious, glorious field for adventure!

CHAPTER IX

At the Monkey Temple

IN MADRAS the Americans made a brief stop to see the Seven Pagodas. They strolled leisurely past great lily ponds and through sandy commons and underbrush to the boulder temples of the once-great city of Bali. The sculptured, impressive temples with their guardians of stone lions, elephants, and bulls rewarded them for the overnight trip on the coal barge which they had had to endure to reach the sacred spot. They walked for a mile through a plantation of young fir trees and came out on the hard sand beach. Pillars and columns stood far out into the water and a line of breakers marked the spot where, their guide told them, still stand other pagodas intact beneath the waves.

The sun was blazing and they sought the mud-and-thatch native village for relief under a cluster of palm trees. The natives pierced green cocoanuts and gave them reviving drinks. Because of the heat they did not care to visit the other ruins but returned to their canal boat, an affair some twenty feet long with a mat roof, side awnings, and a single mast.

The water was asplash with silver drops, and all the afternoon they were cooled by a gentle head-wind. At the edge of darkness was the most beautiful, moist, pink-and-gold sunset they had ever seen.

It was a tiring and unpleasant journey back to Madras but they had the prospect of the clean and comfortable yacht to lure them. The yacht was a splendid sight in the still water of the artificial harbor, sheltered by a breakwater whose long arms were far enough apart to shield a whole fleet of boats.

Watching the twin lighthouses of the harbor fade into the distance Lenora sighed with relief.

"The bedlam of the crowds of coolies on the pier and the bustle of the shops were interesting but I'll never get used to them," she declared, dropping into a comfortable deck chair.

"In four days we should be in Calcutta," Roger said.

"Calcutta is no end interesting," declared Terry.

"It is a good thing Terry has been all these places before and knows his way around," put in Lois. "Otherwise, we should be hopelessly lost."

The boat plowed through the water with ease and grace. There was no hurry. If they did not make Calcutta in four days it did not matter especially. A life of leisure appealed to them after the dust and clamor of the ports at which they stopped.

Early in the morning of their first day out a fine, stinging rain sprang up. It somewhat quelled their spirits, for rain on the water left them with little to do. It was particularly uncomfortable to remain on deck and tiresome to stay in the cabins.

"Hope this storm stops soon," Roger said frowningly at luncheon. "I don't like the wind that is springing up."

"Might be in a fair way for a hurricane," added Terry.

"I thought hurricanes always came suddenly and unannounced," Lois murmured.

"Goody, a hurricane!" Lenora said brightly. "Just what we need to make our voyage complete!"

"A hurricane to sweep us all overboard," agreed Paul.

Roger's fears were soon realized. The fine rain developed into a torrent of fury. Wind and rain swept savagely about the yacht. The sea was swept into angry, destructive waves. The boat tossed fitfully, its powerful engines helpless against the pull of the water.

"If it doesn't stop rocking I'm going to be sick," announced Lenora, her face pale beneath its smile.

"We might all have a chance to see the bottom of the Indian Ocean," added Lois brightly.

"Quiet!" Lenora roared.

"Listen to that wind!" Shirley murmured.

"What was that?" Miss Ernwood asked suddenly as a crash over their heads betokened some mishap.

"Probably our radio," Paul answered.

Roger and Jim in slickers dripping with water entered the cabin and leaned against the door to get their breath.

"One lifeboat has been swept overboard, our radio is out of commission, and the boat is listing heavily to port," Roger announced.

"Oh, Roger, what does it mean?" Shirley asked in an awed whisper.

"It means that the dear old 'Susabella' has a fight on her hands if she wants to remain, as the Chinese say, 'topside'," Lenora answered.

"I'm afraid you're right," Roger said heavily.

"But what can we do, old chap?" Terry asked slowly.

"My suggestion is for us to get busy and bail the water out of the port side," Paul announced vigorously.

"Have you got enough buckets?" Lenora asked, still determinedly cheerful.

The ship gave a sudden lurch that sent them all spinning across the cabin. The floor remained at an angle as the ship did not totally right herself.

Beverly picked herself up from where she had been flung against the ping-pong table as Jim came to her rescue.

"We had better get busy bailing out the water," Terry said, walking unsteadily toward the door.

"It is our only chance," agreed Paul.

The wind was howling and the waves were flinging

themselves upon the boat with devilish glee. Nothing man made could hope to withstand their maniacal fury. The white "Susabella" was tossed about like a toy.

With the Captain and one of the crew at the wheel, the four young men and the remaining sailor proceeded into the hold armed with buckets with which to bail out the water.

The lifeboat which had gone overboard had broken two of the portholes in its flight and now the water poured into the hold faster than the five could dip it up.

The sky was as black as evening but with no friendly stars or moon. Rain-filled clouds lowered over the sea. Green and white-capped mountains of water spilled over the deck and beat unmercifully upon the sturdy little vessel.

As if the elements of storm were not enough to contend with, tragedy struck again. The powerful engine faltered and stopped.

The passengers waited fearfully for the quiet throb of the motor to start again but it did not.

"Now we are in a mess," Lenora groaned.

"The way we are being tossed around, perhaps we'll land at the South Pole instead of Calcutta," Lois added. "Whoops!" she murmured as she steadied herself against the wall.

"Where is Woo Fong?" Beverly asked.

"He should make coffee or something hot to keep up the spirits of us and the boys," agreed Lois.

"It must be hard work shoveling water," Lenora murmured.

Beverly and Shirley donned slickers and went out into the corridor. A volume of green water rolled down the companionway upon them. They waded ankle deep in water into the tiny kitchen presided over by Woo Fong.

"Woo!" Beverly called. "Woo!"

"Yes, Missy," Woo said with a sickly grin. He huddled fearfully between his icebox and the wall.

"Velly bad lain," he said.

"A very bad rain," Beverly agreed, suppressing a laugh at the cook's terrified appearance.

Woo's round yellow face was taut and drawn with fear. His hands were hidden in voluminous sleeves. For the past hour he must have been calling upon all his worthy ancestors to rescue him from this terrible "lain."

"How would you like to see New York, Woo?" Shirley said cheerfully. "Broadway with its millions of lights and trolley cars?" she continued.

"Trying to make him homesick?" Beverly murmured.

"New Yawk velly fine place," Woo bowed, extricating himself from the tiny space into which he had fled. "Woo like tlolley cahs."

"Remember the good coffee you used to make in New York?" Shirley continued. "Make some now—and some sandwiches."

"Light away quick," Woo agreed.

"You can certainly handle the Orientals," Beverly laughed as they went back to the lounge. "Poor Woo was scared to death."

"I don't want to be shipwrecked in India," Lenora was declaring vigorously.

"Who's going to be shipwrecked?" Lois asked in a tired voice. "I merely said it would give you a chance to see the country firsthand."

"I haven't heard the wind howling now for about five minutes," Shirley said suddenly. "Do you suppose it could have stopped?"

"No matter," Lois said. "The engine isn't going yet. We won't be able to move even if the wind has stopped."

"But we won't be showered with rain every second either," Lenora put in. "I'm going on deck and see."

"Better stay here," advised Shirley. "You might be dragged overboard like the lifeboat."

"I'll hang onto something," Lenora promised.

But there was no need. The wind was abating and with it the fury departed from the waves. The water still lapped the white hull as though seeking to draw the "Susabella" beneath the surface, but most of the power was gone.

Woo served his coffee and sandwiches and, with the necessity for bailing the water out of the boat gone, the attention of everyone on board could turn to the damaged engine. It soon became apparent that no permanent repair could be made at the present time. However, the engine was forced into enough power to set the ship in motion again.

Days later the "Susabella" limped over the shoals and quicksand into the mouth of the Ganges and up the sacred, muddy stream to Calcutta.

Repairs were started immediately upon the yacht while the passengers embarked to a hotel at which to live during their stay.

Calcutta, if they expected to see a richly splendid oriental city, disappointed them. The life there was the life of another London. Glittering electric lights, automobiles whizzing by; only the swift tropic night and glorious sunshine were different.

Lenora especially was anxious to be moving. It was finally decided, since the yacht would not be ready to sail for days yet, that they would travel by railway to Benares.

They found the railroad cars even worse than their deplorable hotel room had been. Springless, dusty cars, with bare floors and hard, leather-covered seats and rattling windows, took the joy from their venture. After sundown it grew cold in the dimly lighted box-like affairs.

Benares, the sacred city, was literally the melting pot of all India. The sick came to visit the ghats and bathe in the holy water of Mother Ganges. It was the hiding and breeding place of criminals, the hatching place of conspiracies.

What impressed Lenora were the fakirs, ragged, unkempt, ash-smeared objects that seemed hardly human. Their attitudes and positions which they chose to "acquire merit" were sometimes ludicrous, such as the prize fakir of them all who had all his bones painted in white outline on his brown skin. As Lenora remarked, it was like looking at a group of circus freaks.

On three consecutive mornings they rose by starlight and drove through streets that were hazy with frost to the riverbanks, where the rising sun made rich palaces and temples of the grimy whitewashed buildings of sandstone and adobe. The glory of the sun was reflected in the thousands of believers who came early in the morning to worship. It was the greatest human spectacle in India, this extraordinary manifestation of religious zeal, and also of superstition, and lasted for several hours.

Three times they drove two miles, through empty cantonment streets and crowded native thoroughfares to reach the ghats, or broad staircases, leading to the water's edge. It was worth all their trouble to see the picturesque sweep of the city front with its high cliffs with palaces, temples, and gardens clinging to terraced embankments. It was as surprising and amazing each time they saw it as it had been the first time. It was incredible, dream-like, that so many people came to worship at the rising of the sun. It was as if the keynote of India were revealed here.

Terry procured a boat and they were rowed slowly up and down the three-mile river front. After they had gone the length of the ghats they landed where the crowd was thickest and the din the loudest. There were priests, fakirs, pilgrims, beggars, jugglers, snake charmers, money changers and idlers.

That afternoon they visited the Monkey Temple at Durga. The sight was appalling—a red sandstone court where the priests waited for gifts and gray apes with red faces sat in rows on the parapets, roofs, and swarmed up and down columns. One dropped down noiselessly beside Lenora and stretched a long, lean, gray arm over her shoulder to grasp at her necklace.

Needless to say, Lenora let out a scream that effectively chased the offending monkey.

Lois giggled unfeelingly. "Look, he is making a face at you!"

Lenora was not impressed.

The big apes were chattering and making faces and the little ones ran to safety. However, as the apes became more and more numerous and their curiosity grew and they came closer, the tourists fled.

Once in safety Lenora could breathe more easily.

"Let's go back to Calcutta," she proposed. "I can cope more easily with trolley cars and automobiles."

"You wanted to see India," Lois laughed. "Now you are seeing it."

"Where's Beverly?" Shirley was the one who asked.

"Last time I saw her she was trying to get one of

the monkeys to pose while she took his picture," Paul smiled.

"I'll go back for her," Jim said and departed forthwith.

He was gone so long the others decided they had better go back in a body for their errant members. But their search was unrewarded. Neither Beverly nor Jim was to be seen.

"That's funny," murmured Roger. "Perhaps we had better wait in the car."

"Yes, it is only a question of days until they return," sighed Lenora.

Lenora had no idea, when she made her flippant remark, how near she was to being correct, for Beverly and Jim were in trouble again.

Beverly, absorbed in her picture-taking possibilities, had wandered farther from her friends than was prudent here in such surroundings. Becoming conscious of the fact that she was alone, she looked up suddenly to find her friends. They were disappearing around the corner of the temple, going back to the car she presumed.

Busy closing her folding camera Beverly took a few steps after them. A voice broke across her thoughts and a shadow blotted out the sunshine on the path ahead of her. Before she looked up she knew who it was.

During the weeks that had passed since they had seen Count Alexis in the merchant's shop in Agra Beverly had almost forgotten him and the curious map, half of which was still in Jim's possession. Too, she had forgotten the menace of the Count's determination to secure that portion of map.

"We meet again, Miss Gray," he said with a slight bow.

Though she had been startled at his sudden appearance and her heart was beating uncomfortably fast, Beverly strove to appear perfectly calm as she looked up. She thought fleetingly that Lenora would somehow humorously tie the fact of the Count's presence and the Monkey Temple together. A fitting place to meet him, as it were.

Beverly merely nodded and made as though to pass on. The Count was not to be avoided, however. He stepped in front of her.

"So sorry to detain you, but there is a little matter of, shall we say, unfinished business to attend to. Where could we find a more opportune spot? We are entirely alone."

Beverly smiled. "Ah, but we are not alone. My friends are waiting for me."

"They shall wait until I have what I want," he said imperturbably.

"There, too, you are wrong. They will not wait. They will come after me," she informed him confidently.

Count Alexis drew a small, business-like automatic revolver from his pocket.

"I think I can deal very well with anyone who might come," he said, his teeth sparkling in a smile.

Beverly, with difficulty, quelled a sudden nervous jumping of her heart and smiled also.

"You may as well put that away. You don't frighten me. There is no cause for dramatics."

"You are wrong, my young friend. There is a need of dramatics or anything else that will secure for me the map which you have."

"Unfortunately, we have but half of a map. However, we will sell it to you," Beverly said brightly.

He regarded her suspiciously but her gaze was guileless.

"What is your price?"

"A million dollars," Beverly said quietly, confidently.

That ought to hold him, she thought. If anyone was foolish enough to pay a millon dollars for a scrap of apparently worthless paper he must be crazy.

"You Americans are fond of joking," he said. "But I am more serious. If you have not the whole map the half is quite as important to me. But such a price is out of the question. You will be glad enough to give it to me for nothing. At least your friends will," he said.

"What do you mean?" she asked sharply.

"It should be a cheap price for your safe return." He bowed.

Fortunately at that moment Beverly saw Jim's tall figure coming round the corner of the temple. He had evidently come in search of her. She waved and he answered her gesture.

"The gods are kind to me today," Count Alexis said, smiling. "It is the young Monsieur Stanton himself. As I remember, he is the young man who actually has the map in his possession."

It was then Beverly realized what Jim was walking nonchalantly into. She tried to gesture him away.

"I must ask you to do nothing to warn him," the Count said, his revolver once more in prominence.

Beverly was forced to stand helplessly to one side, apparently at ease, while Jim walked nearer and nearer to them. He was unaware of anything amiss and from a distance he could not recognize the Count, although he had seen him on more than one occasion.

"Beverly, we thought you were lost—— Hullo!" He whistled in amazement, his gaze on the revolver in the man's hand. Then his eyes traveled slowly to the Count's face. "Well, well," he said with a grin. "An old friend! Have you come to live permanently among the monkeys, Count?"

"Such is not the case," the Count said, smiling. "I would advise you not to try anything foolish, my friend."

Jim's grin widened. He had been contemplating knocking the gun from the Count's hand. Now he shoved his hands into his pockets and waited for the next move.

"I suggest we go to my car and on to a place where we can talk undisturbed," the Count advised. He shifted the revolver suggestively. "I am considered an excellent marksman, but I trust there will be no need for a demonstration."

Beverly looked at Jim as he took her arm and they walked ahead of the Count to where an automobile with a native driver waited.

The Hindu stood at the door while Jim and Beverly and the Count got into the rear seat. Beverly had only a fleeting glimpse of the lean, brown face beneath the folds of a white turban. It struck a reminiscent chord in her memory. But then, she supposed, nearly all Hindus look alike to an inexperienced eye.

The Count spoke fleetingly in Hindustani to the driver and the Hindu took his place at the wheel. The car leaped forward, jolting the occupants unmercifully.

"Nice country, India," Jim said conversationally. He appeared at his ease, even to be enjoying the situation. Yet Beverly knew that underneath his ease he was searching for a means of escape. "Yes, sir," Jim continued. "A nice country—snakes, crocodiles, monkeys——"

"Nothing personal in that remark, I trust," the Count said with a flash of humor.

In the mirror over the driver Beverly caught a pair of dark eyes fixed on her with inscrutable intensity. When she saw them, the gaze was immediately averted. Why did she persist in thinking the man was familiar? Had she seen him somewhere before? During the past weeks she had seen countless Hindus. He might be almost any one of them. Yet he impressed her vaguely as being someone she had known a long time ago.

The car was ascending a narrow, dusty road toward a mountain top. Suddenly there was a popping report and a long-drawn-out hiss.

A flat tire! It gave the prisoners a brief respite from whatever was in store for them. Jim could not suppress, wholly, his delight.

The Count was annoyed and poured his wrath upon the head of his driver. The Hindu shrugged his shoulders and remained passively silent.

Beverly had been thinking fast and furiously on the brief ride, searching for a plan by which she and Jim could escape from the Count. Quite by accident her eyes had fallen on the ring on her hand. Twice Omar El Hamel's gift had proved particularly helpful in extricating her from difficult situations. Would it help now? They needed help now as they had not needed it before. There was no telling where the Count was taking them or what would happen once they arrived there. If anything was to be done, it must needs be done before they reached their destination. The Count might have many friends where he was taking them, and against numbers they did not stand a chance.

They were forced to get out of the car while the driver changed the tire. In descending, Beverly stumbled off the running-board and caught at the impassive brown Hindu to steady herself. Only an instant did the white hand rest in the brown one, but it was enough. In that instant Beverly transferred all her hopes of their rescue. When she straightened up her ring was in the possession of the impassive driver. Only a gleam of light from his dark eyes showed her that he understood. Now if only he proved as impressed by the ring as the other natives had——

Working without haste the Hindu finally got the spare tire on the car and they were ready to proceed. They climbed back into the car as they had been before. Once more the Hindu was impassive behind the wheel.

Beverly's hopes began to dwindle. Evidently the ring meant nothing to him. If he was going to help them surely he would have done something before they returned to the car!

Her hand lay idly on the seat and she felt it grasped in Jim's warm one. She was glad of his comforting pressure.

"It is a very nice tour you are taking us on, Count," Jim said, smiling. "Might I ask what is the purpose of it?"

"The purpose is to secure what is rightfully mine," the Count said.

"Why go to all this trouble?" Jim was purposefully innocent. "If we have anything that belongs to you we shall gladly give it to you."

"I refer to the map entrusted to your care by an English sailor," the Count said. "It was intended for me."

Jim shook his head. "Sorry to disappoint you. Slim,

the English sailor, gave it to me and I intend to keep it. I dare say it is safe enough in Calcutta."

"Calcutta!" The word escaped the Count with all the unexpectedness of a pistol shot.

"Calcutta," Jim repeated. Then he smiled. "My dear chap, you don't think I carry it around with me?"

"We shall soon see," the Count replied, once more his suave self. "Omar! What the devil is the matter?"

The car halted. Slowly the driver turned round in his seat. The round hole of a revolver appeared over the back of the seat.

"If the Sahib will drop his automatic——" a smooth voice intimated. "Now if the Mem-sahib will pick it up?"

As the Count's gun thudded on the floor, Beverly reached down and secured it. The Count's face was ludicrous with amazement.

"Omar, what do you mean by this?" he thundered.

"Omar?" Beverly said in surprise, a sudden gate opening in her memory. "Omar?" she repeated. She leaned forward. "Are you Omar El Hamel?"

"It is so, Mem-sahib."

"Then it was your ring that I gave you back there! The one you gave to me in New York."

"Then I said you would someday come to my country," the Hindu acknowledged. "Time has been most gracious to the Mem-sahib."

"Will you please tell me what this is all about?"

Jim demanded. "It is all very delightful that you now have the Count's gun, but——"

"Everything will be okey-doke now," Beverly assured him. In a few brief words she explained her relationship with Omar and of giving him her ring a few minutes back.

They had stopped on a road which was barren. Dusty, flat, treeless, and uninhabited, the ground stretched away for miles.

"If the Sahib will get out," Omar said, motioning toward the Count.

His plan pleased Jim immensely. The young American took the Count's gun from Beverly.

"Move, Count, I'm a pretty good marksman myself."

With his dignity sorely ruffled, his face dark with rage, but speechless, the Count got out of the car and stood on the road, watching them.

"I'll watch him, Omar. You start the car and turn it around."

"It is so, Sahib," Omar acknowledged.

With a roar, the engine responded. Omar turned the car in the direction from which they had come. Through the back window Beverly and Jim watched the Count's solitary figure fade in the distance.

"And it is a long walk to Benares," Beverly said laughingly.

"How did the Mem-sahib meet the evil one?" Omar wanted to know as the car sped over the road.

"In London," Beverly answered readily. "I thought

he was perfectly respectable. I even thought he was
quite nice at first."

"It is unfortunate," Omar said slowly.

"This afternoon he met me at the Monkey
Temple."

"The Mem-sahib will do well to leave India,"
Omar advised. "The danger lies not only in this one
man but in a group who want much gold to further
their evil ends."

"You know him well, Omar?" Beverly asked.

"I know him, Mem-sahib, but I also know many
men."

"Did you ever hear of anyone called Black Barney?" Beverly wanted to know next.

"It is so," Omar nodded. "The two evil ones are as
brothers."

"But——" Beverly was at a loss. "Do you remember, Jim, that time in Cairo the Count said Barney
was not his friend?"

"Omar has seen them much together," the Hindu
put in.

"Are they both here in India—I mean, is Barney
here, too?" Jim asked excitedly.

"Yes, Sahib."

Jim whistled expressively. "Then this is no place
for us!"

"No, Sahib," agreed the Hindu.

CHAPTER X

China

"It DOESN'T look like so very much," Lenora said finally.

The eight young people were bent attentively over the ping-pong table in the lounge of the yacht. Jim had spread out the piece of paper on which was drawn a crude attempt at a map. It was the same map which was causing so much trouble with Count Alexis.

Omar El Hamel had driven Jim and Beverly back to Benares and then taken himself off into the wilds of India again. After explaining where they had been Beverly and Jim urged the others to return to Calcutta, and, once there, repair work on the yacht was hurried to an end, and they set sail once more.

Now Lenora had given her verdict after a careful scrutiny of the paper which other people valued so highly as to be willing to do almost anything to secure it.

"It is rather the worse for wear," Lois agreed.

"There are rather crude lines and I can't figure out what they stand for," Jim said with a frown. "Take these two X's close together here. The second X is much larger than the first. What could that mean?"

"I have it!" Lenora said suddenly. "It must be the solution of a mystery story. X always marks the spot where the body is found."

No one but Lois paid any attention to that remark and she only gave her friend a scathing glance.

"There is a sketch here," Terry indicated the spot with his finger, "that might be anything from a house to a horse."

"Read what is written on the back again," Beverly requested.

"Just four words," Jim murmured. "Fiji, inland, Temple, and pillar. They make no sense whatever."

"With the other half of the map it probably would," Paul pointed out.

"Therefore, to get the treasure we either have to give this map to the Count or secure the other half for ourselves."

"The mysterious Barney person has the other half, is that right?" Terry asked.

Jim nodded. "That is what Slim said in his note."

"We don't even know what he looks like," Shirley said.

"We should plan a campaign to get the other half

of the map away from Barney," Lenora said brightly.

"Can you tell us where to start?" Lois wanted to know.

"I'll go and ask the scarab I got in Egypt. Perhaps it can help us."

"I wish you would get rid of that thing," Lois frowned. "Send it back to Egypt or throw it overboard."

"Why?" Lenora asked innocently.

"Hasn't it caused us enough trouble already? First Beverly gets lost in India when the river boat upset, then we nearly all drown in a hurricane, and now the Count is popping up again. I'm telling you it has brought nothing but bad luck."

"Everything you mention is so," Lenora conceded. "But haven't they all turned out all right in the end? I don't believe the scarab has anything to do with it," she declared, "and I intend to take it home with me!"

"At that rate we can look forward to a very interesting visit in China," Lois sighed.

Despite the others' laughs, Lois persisted in her gloomy presentiment.

"I can hardly wait to get to Canton," Shirley said. "I want to buy a jade necklace."

"I've heard such a lot about China I'm all thrilled," Lenora declared.

"It's nice to hear of it," Terry grinned, "but I agree with the proverb which says 'One seeing is better than a thousand people telling you of it.'"

"No one can do it justice," agreed Miss Ern-wood.

At Singapore they had their first glimpse of the land of a thousand mysteries. The water front was swarming with Chinese. The native quarter was a mass of yelling yellow men, buying, selling, gambling, eating, and even sleeping. There were outdoor restaurants at the long tables of which the coolies were busy with bowls and chopsticks.

Woo Fong disappeared for the whole day the boat was anchored there. His round, shiny face was wreathed in smiles when he returned and it was evident that he had enjoyed his return to the country of his ancestors.

"On to Hong Kong!" Lenora cried, waving to no one in particular on the dock.

Lois sighed. "I am going below and practice using chopsticks. I don't think I'll ever be adept at it."

"We'll get Woo Fong to teach us," Lenora proposed.

Accordingly the two went off full of enthusiasm for this latest proposal. Terry and Paul followed after a while to criticize the performance.

Jim and Roger went to confer with the Captain. Miss Ernwood went down to her cabin to write letters, and that left Shirley and Beverly alone on deck.

The girls curled up in comfortable chairs.

"I was thinking," Shirley murmured, "isn't it about time for a reunion of the Alpha Deltas?"

Beverly nodded and smiled. "It would be rather difficult with us halfway across the world."

"I'd like to see them all again," Shirley continued dreamily.

"Getting homesick?" Beverly wanted to know.

Shirley nodded unabashed. "Terribly! I want Broadway, millions of lights, and——"

"And a part in a new play," Beverly finished for her. "You're homesick for work, aren't you?"

Shirley laughed. "Strange, isn't it? But I'm afraid by the time we return home Dale Arden will be forgotten."

Beverly shook her head. "No. Dale Arden won't be forgotten. Oh, I don't mean because of what happened that night in New York when you were ill. Dale Arden will be remembered because she was a great little actress. When she returns it will be in new health and well-equipped to take up her career where she left off."

"I hope so," Shirley sighed.

"I've got it!" Lenora said gleefully, dashing up the companionway to them. "Watch!"

Laboriously and with infinite care she proceeded to demonstrate her newly acquired ability with chopsticks. But she fumbled. One of the sticks fell to the deck.

"Doggone it," she exploded. "Now I've got to practice some more!"

"Ha, ha!" Lois enjoyed her friend's failure.

"Let's see you do it," proposed Lenora.

"All right."

Lois proceeded to demonstrate her ability, but, sadly, she was no better than Lenora.

"I can't understand it," she said in a puzzled voice. "It looked so easy when Woo Fong did it."

The nights on board ship as they sailed slowly up the China Sea were warm and starlighted. Games were enjoyed by all. When possible there was dancing on the deck. That was enjoyed most of all.

"This is the life," Lenora sighed. She was stretched out comfortably in a deck chair, a glass of cool lemonade in one hand and a sandwich in the other.

"If Lenora doesn't weigh two hundred pounds when this voyage is over it will be a miracle," Lois declared from where she was dancing with Paul.

"How so?" Lenora inquired suspiciously.

"Every time I look at you you are eating," was the answer. "You don't exercise it off either."

Lenora made a face at her and smiled sweetly at Terry.

"Will you love me when I'm fat?" she wanted to know.

Terry raised his hands in mock sorrow.

"Positively not! I shall join the Foreign Legion to forget," he confided somberly.

Lenora frowned thoughtfully. She eyed the lunch in her hands and then Terry.

"It is too bad, really, because I don't think you would make a very good soldier," Lenora said, complacently munching her sandwich.

Up in the bow where they stood watching the boat cut through the water, Jim and Beverly heard the gale of laughter that came from the others.

"Our trip has been a fine success, hasn't it?" she murmured.

"I've enjoyed every minute of it—except when we came back from that hunting trip in India and found you were lost," Jim replied.

"What was it Omar said when he said good-by to us in Benares?" she murmured. "Do you remember?"

"Wasn't it 'May heavenly incense perfume your dream, and celestial music bring you the rapture of profound peace'?"

"I like the flowery speeches of the Orient," Beverly laughed. She continued in a more serious vein: "Shirley said she was homesick the other day. She wants to go back and get into another play. I'd rather like to see the United States again myself."

"Aren't you having a good time?" he asked in surprise.

"The best ever!" she declared instantly. "One good thing about it is that I have my work right with me. On nights like this I could write and write and——"

Jim laughed. "You came on this trip for a vacation and you've worked more than the rest of us all put together."

"I sent Charlie Blaine two articles on India from Calcutta," she said. "I hope he prints them."

"He will," Jim laughed cheerfully. "Haven't you heard? A certain Miss Beverly Gray is considered a very promising writer. I have it on good authority that her latest book is a wow. In fact——"

Beverly pressed her fingers against his lips.

"Stop it! Do you want to make me conceited?" she demanded gaily.

"Why, after a while," he continued as her fingers were hastily withdrawn when he kissed them, "you will be dining with royalty. The President will invite you to live at the White House and you will look at some certain people and say 'Oh, yes, I faintly remember them. I believe I went round the world with them at one time. I don't know how it happened——' "

"You should be thrown overboard for even thinking such things," she said severely. "You know perfectly well I shall never forget my friends. Success wouldn't be worth anything without all of you——"

"Don't," he whispered, suddenly serious, "ever forget that there is a young fellow, really not such a bad sort"—with a flash of humor—"who loves you very dearly."

"I shan't forget," she answered in a low, husky voice. She blinked rapidly to clear away a sudden mist that obscured the stars.

"He couldn't give you diamonds or fancy yachts," Jim continued, his cheek against her hair, "but he'll always be around when you want him."

"Diamonds aren't everything and I never did want to own a yacht," she said very low. "If the young man——"

"Good night everybody!" Lenora's voice broke between them and a chorus answered her.

Beverly brought herself down from the moonbeam where she felt she had been walking. There seemed to be a sudden chill in the air and she shivered.

"It is getting late, Jim, and we reach Hong Kong in the morning."

"Yes," he agreed slowly. "I suppose we should join the others."

They greeted Hong Kong eagerly. The girls were at the rail on deck long before the yacht dropped anchor in the harbor. They wanted to miss none of the thrill of arrival in a strange and unknown port.

For their first, comprehensive view of the city they went up to the Peak, the crest of the hill overlooking the city. From there they had a full view of the harbor and the boats lying at anchor.

The center of the town was mostly European. Along Wyndham Hill Road (Flower Street) the roads were banked solid with baskets of the native gardeners. The girls went back to the boat with huge armfuls of yellow and white narcissus.

The next morning they crossed the bay to Canton.

"I thought Canton was situated on a river," Lenora said, looking at the crowded harbor.

"So it is," Terry nodded.

"Well, where's the water?" Lenora wanted to know.

The shore line was a mass of Chinese river-craft, junks that looked like piled firewood. Poles, with lines stretched across holding the family wash, stuck up grotesquely. So tightly were the boats wedged together there was no water visible.

"Two hundred thousand people live on the water in those boats," Terry informed them. "The boats called Flower Boats are really restaurants and, believe me, there is a gay night life on them. The boats don't all belong to poor people, either. Many rich men entertain at costly dinners on the Flower Boats."

"Is it true a Chinese dinner lasts seven hours?" Lois wanted to know.

"Seven hours!" Lenora gasped. "I think I'll move to China. Just think, life would be practically one glorious meal."

Terry laughed. "Yes," he said. "The Chinese royal dinner starts with nuts and ends with soup and then starts all over again. They have about everything from sharks' fins to a hundred-year-old egg."

"An egg a hundred years old?" Shirley was amazed.

"Here in China they have egg cemeteries. You can have an egg as old as you wish."

"Is there much difference in the fifty-year-old and one-hundred-year-old eggs?" Lenora wanted to know.

Lois shivered. "I don't think I'll eat any eggs while I'm here. Somebody might slip in a new one on me."

In the streets, through which they rode in rickshas,

they saw barefoot coolies balancing everything from
live pigs to dried fish on their shoulder poles. The in-
congruousness of the names of the streets pleased
their sense of humor. They found in Peace Street
a perfect turmoil that belied the name. The Street of
Nine-Fold Brightness was dark; and the Street of
Refreshing Breezes, close and warm.

"Queer people, these Chinese," Lenora commented.

"They think we are just as queer," Lois said dryly.

"They might entertain such ideas about you of
course," Lenora acknowledged. "But me——"

She was abruptly halted in her speech by Terry
yanking her after him as he followed Shirley and
Roger into a shop in Jade Street.

Shirley still sought her jade necklace and earrings.
They found exquisite pieces from which to choose
but they were all so splendid she had a difficult time
making up her mind.

Here in the shops with their exquisite silks and
jade and teakwood the young people felt an urge to
buy at least half of what they saw.

Shirley bought herself a necklace and Beverly a
bracelet of the green spheres dazzling to look at.
Lenora secured earrings which, she proudly asserted,
made her feel like a duchess. Lois disdained jewels in
favor of a tiny brass horse guaranteed to bring good
luck. She felt it would counteract any evil influence
from Lenora's prized scarab.

The shopkeeper placed his left hand in his right,

bowed low, and shook hands with himself in bidding them farewell.

The streets were crowded, wares openly displayed, and over the doorway of each shop a flag-like affair printed in Chinese figures.

"What do they say?" Lenora asked Terry.

"That one says 'Ten Thousand Times Successful' and another says 'Heavenly Happiness'——"

"How do you know? You don't speak Chinese!" Lenora said suspiciously.

"My friend in Shanghai told me," Terry said loftily.

"When are we going to lunch?" Lenora wanted to know.

"My sweet, we will go to lunch in just the time it would take a lark to swallow a grasshopper."

"How long is that?" Lenora demanded.

"A Chinese instant," Terry laughed.

The only trouble the young people had that day was when Lenora started to take pictures. A curious crowd gathered, effectively blocking all traffic.

"Why do we think of China as so different from our country?" Lenora asked as they were returning to the yacht. "They have almost everything we have in their cities—trolley cars—policemen—bicycles——"

"Do we go on to Shanghai immediately?" Roger put in.

"Let's stay here for a couple of days," Lois and Lenora proposed together.

"And then let's go down the Si River a little way and see what the country is like," suggested the other girls.

So it was agreed that they should linger a little longer, exploring Canton.

CHAPTER XI

Pirates

BACK IN NEW YORK in the apartment in Mrs. Callahan's establishment four girls were busy with various occupations. Connie Elwood was pasting newspaper clippings into a scrapbook. Kathleen Ryan was composing a letter to her friends across the sea. Hope Rodgers was busy with pencil and paper figuring accounts from the gownshop she and Lenora had started in partnership. The remaining member of the quartette, Virginia Harris, was reading a magazine.

The girls, with the exception of Hope, whom they had met only when they came to New York, were all members of the famous Alpha Delta society which had formed while the girls were students at Vernon College.

Connie was studying fashion designing while Kathleen, almost as irrepressible and fun-loving as Lenora, had lately entered an Interior Decorating establishment. Virginia Harris had arrived in New York only the day before on a short vacation from her medical studies in Chicago.

"I wish all the girls could have been here for our annual reunion," Connie sighed, looking up from her work.

"By rights, we shouldn't have it until June," Kathleen put in.

"Even then all of us probably couldn't make it," Virginia smiled. "I shall be hard at work in June. I must take a vacation when I can get it. By the way, have any of you heard from the world travelers?"

"I had a letter yesterday from Beverly," Connie said. "She mailed it in Calcutta. They must be having a marvelous time. Would you like to read it?"

The girls exchanged the news each had acquired during the months they had not seen Virginia. They were deep in discussion when the telephone in the hall rang.

"I'll get it," Kathleen sang out.

The telephone, used by most of the household, was outside the girls' door and now Kathleen left the door ajar as she lifted the receiver.

"Who is it?" Connie stuck her head out.

"I wonder if somebody is playing tricks on us," Kathleen said in mystification. "The operator said it was China calling."

"China!" Connie gasped in amazement.

"Do you owe a laundry bill?" Kathleen asked with a grin. "Oooo——" She held the receiver away from her ear. "Listen to all the funny noises."

Their conversation brought Virginia and Hope onto the scene.

"Yes! Hullo——" Kathleen spoke excitedly into the receiver. "She, the operator, keeps saying 'China calling, hold the line, please!' If she doesn't tell me who it is I'll jump in the telephone," Kathleen declared, hopping up and down in excitement.

"Hul-hullo! Who? Lenora! Say, are you calling all the way from China? Well, you don't have to yell!"

"Ask them what's new," Lois advised her friend.

Lenora grinned at them. "She said I was yelling. It doesn't seem possible that we're talking across the ocean."

"Well, talk to her," Lois prodded her. "Or let me."

In the brief time allotted to them the girls all managed to say a word to their friends so far away in New York. Afterward the little exchange of greetings lingered long in their hearts.

It was the last morning they intended to spend in Canton and each seemed to have something different to do. Lois and Lenora went off to Jade Street again.

"We'll be back to the yacht in time for tiffin," Lenora promised.

The others scattered, but shortly before lunch they appeared one after the other at the "Susabella" —that is, all but Lois and Lenora.

"I hope they aren't lost," Shirley said, scanning the dock for sight of her friends.

"I told Lenora she shouldn't go off alone," Terry commented. "Perhaps we should go after them."

"They'll turn up," Roger said confidently. "Lenora is probably arguing over the price of something with a shopkeeper."

"I'll wager Connie and Kathleen were surprised when we talked to them this morning," Shirley said, curling up in a deck chair.

"We had a reunion with them after all," Beverly agreed. "Interesting, wasn't it? Across all those miles of ocean and land we talked to them as though they were in the same room with us."

"It helps to keep in touch——"

"Here they come," Jim said from the rail. "They are certainly in a rush!"

"Pull in the anchor! Start the motor!" Lenora cried as she climbed aboard.

"We've got to get out of here right away!" added Lois breathlessly.

"What's the matter?" Shirley asked.

Lenora sank into a chair and fanned herself with her hat.

"Roger, tell the Captain to start right away! We can't stay here."

"Did you rob a bank?" Roger asked laughingly.

"Don't stand there doing nothing." Lois joined Lenora in her pleas for immediate departure. "We've got to go."

"But why?" Beverly demanded. "We can sail after lunch."

"But we can't wait," Lenora protested.

"Either give a good reason or forget it," Paul sighed.

"Count Alexis is in Canton!" Lenora burst her bombshell.

"What?" Both Jim and Beverly were on their feet.

"We saw him in the Street of Tailors," Lenora nodded.

"Did he see you?" Beverly asked intently.

"He couldn't help it," Lois said. "Lenora bumped into him and almost knocked him over."

"Did he know you?" Jim wanted to know.

"We didn't wait to see," Lenora laughed.

"We took one look at him and ran," Lois giggled. "He must have thought we were completely mad."

"He must remember you from Paris and Switzerland," Beverly said with a frown. "He is certainly close on our trail."

"How does it happen he knows just where we will be?" Shirley asked.

The warm color flooded Beverly's cheeks. "When we were friends, in Switzerland and Paris and London, I often mentioned the places we wanted to see."

"All he has to do is go there and find us," added Lenora brightly. "Do we sail right away?"

"Right away!" Roger acknowledged and went off to give orders to that effect.

While the young people lunched the boat made slow progress down the Si River. After tiffin they went on deck to watch the shore line and the scenes that drifted past. They passed numerous Chinese junks, with their square lateen sails, and native houseboats moving only as the boatmen waded or walked along the riverbank and pulled them.

On the riverbank, kneeling in the water, were women washing clothes. Rice fields, interrupted by silver ribbons which were canals or tiny rivers, stretched away for miles.

Suddenly over the crest of a hill would rise a pagoda with its queer slanting roof upturned at the corners. From a temple close to the riverbank came the faint, discordant tinkle of Chinese music and the solemn pealing of a gong. They could almost scent the faint incense from the brazier before the altar.

The men on many of the little junks they passed glared at them reproachfully as if resenting this invasion of their native habitat.

Beverly had established her typewriter on a low stool before her chair and as they idly drifted along she wrote little tidbits of what they saw.

The afternoon passed peacefully enough. For the most part they were all busy comparing their purchases in Canton or making up their minds to whom at home to give what.

"Do you suppose Kathleen would like this little ivory elephant?" Lenora asked, puzzled.

"What use would she have for it?" Lois demanded. She had intended to give Kathleen something similar so it was up to her to persuade Lenora to give their friend something else.

"She might use it to scare the mice," Lenora suggested helpfully.

"We don't have any mice in the apartment," Beverly interrupted.

"Then I'll take her some pet white mice," Lenora beamed.

"You will not!" Lois said firmly. "I refuse to live with anyone's mice."

"You shouldn't object if the mice don't," Lenora giggled. "I suppose I will have to get Kathleen something else when we get to Shanghai and keep this elephant for myself."

The Eastern night came on rapidly and the sky at sunset was a riot of color; long shafts of red and gold melted indiscriminately into blue and violet.

The scene could not fail to inspire Lois' artistic heart and out came her sketching pencil and block. Long after the colors had faded Lois remained on deck sketching, filling in from her memory. So absorbed was she even dinner could not lure her away.

Since the others did not propose to dine without her it made the situation rather awkward, especially for Lenora. That worthy sat herself on the top step of the companionway and proceeded to annoy Lois.

"Lois, please!" Lenora begged finally. "Do you want to see me waste away to a shadow?"

"Go down and have your dinner," Lois said, frowning over her work. "I'll join you in a few minutes."

"If you don't come now I shall eat both our dinners," Lenora declared and disappeared.

Lois considered that. It was quite possible, for Lenora was capable of it. Therefore, she decided to avert such a catastrophe and put her work aside with a sigh.

Dinner was a hilarious affair, as was usual when they were all in high spirits. Not a shadow of coming events disturbed them. If they had known to what fate the "Susabella" was carrying them they might not have been so carefree.

After dinner Lenora and Terry got out the chessboard and proceeded to lose themselves in the game. Miss Ernwood retired to write letters, as did Lois and Paul. Roger was busy conferring with the Captain on their proposed route. It left Jim, Beverly, and Shirley alone on deck.

The young people were chatting pleasantly, not paying the slightest heed to other craft on the river, when a sudden explosion shattered the serenity of the night air. As if that were the signal, tumult arose as shadowy figures loomed over the rail of the yacht.

Silently, under cover of the darkness, a Chinese boat had drawn alongside of the "Susabella" and now her crew swarmed onto the American boat.

"Pirates!" Jim said under his breath.

The attack was a complete surprise. Before the three on deck could do or say a thing they were surrounded by evil-looking men with rifles while some of the same sort went down the companionway. They heard a scream, probably from Lenora.

They had heard that boats were sometimes at-

tacked by river pirates in this sector. But they had
never supposed that such a thing could happen to
them. It had been the farthest thought from their
minds.

"What—what will they do?" Shirley shivered.

"Take anything of value," Jim said viciously. "If
I could only——"

Three men remained with the Americans on deck
while the others scrambled down the hatchway after
their leader. It did not take long for the Chinese to
reappear again on deck, scowls on their faces.

"Can't find many jewels," Shirley laughed.

"He doesn't look pleased," Jim said grimly. "It
hasn't been worth much to him to hold us up."

The leader crossed to the three Americans on deck.
Yellow fingers snatched the jade necklace from Shirley's throat before any of them knew what was happening. The same fingers grabbed at the bracelet on
Beverly's wrist.

Without stopping to think of the consequences
Beverly did what her temper dictated. She eluded
him and brought her hand up with a resounding
smack into the pirate's face. Horror-stricken at what
she had done she waited for what would happen.

A heavy silence dropped over all of them. Only
the quiet lapping of the water against the hull could
be heard. Then, surprisingly enough, the pirate chief
smiled—a grimace that held more of a sneer than
humor.

At that smile Beverly's heart almost stopped; then

it raced on rebelliously as the pirate captain spoke sharply to two of his men. His henchmen closed in upon the two girls rapidly. Hardly aware of what was happening, Shirley and Beverly were propelled rapidly toward the side of the boat.

When it finally came home to them that they were being kidnaped they put up a stiff resistance. Jim, too, did not intend to stand idly by and see anything of the sort occur.

Jim swung his fist into the face of the man nearest him. It took the Chinese by surprise and he sprawled on the deck at his leader's feet.

For three Americans up against six pirates they created an uproar. But the outcome was inevitable. In the midst of the melee a shot rang out, strangely muffled.

Beverly's last glimpse of the "Susabella" was of three of the pirates standing over Jim's prostrate form.

CHAPTER XII

Kidnaped

WITH each sway of the boat the smoky oil lamp swung to and fro. Staring at it, Beverly wondered how long it would be before it upset and spilled the oil over everything. Not that it would matter very much! The oil could not ruin anything in the cabin and the darkness would be more or less of a blessing.

In the darkness they would not be able to see the filth of their surroundings or the evil faces of the guards at the door. They would not have to stare at the junk-littered room and compare it with their tidy cabin on the "Susabella."

The two girls had entered this room immediately upon their arrival on the junk and so far had been left to their own devices. To be sure, there were two guards at the door, evil, dirty men, but they made no movement toward the girls. Not by so much as a whisper would the girls have known they were there —unless either of them attempted to go onto the

deck. Their progress would be immediately halted—
by the rifle each man carried. Only two men, but
they formed a perfect barricade to the outside world!

Through the porthole over their head the girls had
been able only to see the blackness of night and
water. Not another sign of life! Overhead on the
deck now and then could be heard a faint footfall or
a voice that sang out suddenly in the queer, singsong,
native tongue.

For hours they had been sitting here on an overturned packing box waiting—waiting—waiting for
what they did not know. Shirley's head was resting
on Beverly's shoulder now and her friend was asleep.

Beverly put a comforting arm about Shirley's
shoulder and frowned at the door. Now that there
seemed to be no immediate danger to them, her
thoughts turned back to those brief, fateful moments on the "Susabella." In her mind's eye she could
again see Jim struggling with the pirates and then
lying so still on the deck. Her heart beat smother-
ingly at each thought of how seriously he might be
hurt. If only she could go to him——

But it was like wishing for the moon. There was
no chance of either her or Shirley leaving the Chinese
junk now. She supposed they would be held for ransom—since that was the usual procedure in such in-
stances. But for how long? And where were they
being taken? With every minute they were leaving
the "Susabella" and their friends and Jim farther and
farther behind. Would they ever see any of them

again? Very often people who disappeared with Chinese pirates never were seen again.

Comforting thought, she told herself sternly. She mustn't think such thoughts! Would news of their disappearance be radioed to all the world? Would the headlines of the *Tribune*—the same headlines she used to hunt!—spread the news of the kidnaping of the "American Actress, Dale Arden, and the Popular Writer, Beverly Gray"? She smiled at her own egotism. She wasn't popular yet! Oh, maybe Connie's newspaper clippings had praised and flattered a little. Still, she was far from the goal she had set for herself. A goal she might never see—now!

Look at the bright side! She mentally chided herself. The bright side—if any! Of course, the boat might suddenly sink and everyone be drowned but her and Shirley. That would solve the problem of the pirates but it would leave them in the middle of the Si River with nothing to hang onto. Besides, it was impossible that such a thing could happen! Boats didn't sink without a reason, and if it did sink, they probably couldn't get out of this cabin!

The guards at the door shifted their positions, only to fall into immobility again. Every time she looked at their rifles she thought of the shot she had heard as they were leaving the "Susabella"—and of Jim. How badly had he been hurt? That thought worried her more than her own precarious position.

Shirley shifted her position a little and murmured: "Jim—Jim——"

Beverly looked down sharply. Shirley was still asleep and in her dream she had called for Jim. What did it mean? Was her imagination running riot or had there been something new and gentle in Shirley's voice? Beverly passed a dazed hand across her eyes. Was it possible that Shirley—and Jim——

But Jim professed to love her, Beverly! In that case—— Beverly shook her head hopelessly. It couldn't be! Was Shirley in love with Jim? Jim was in love with her, Beverly, and she was in love with——

"What's the matter? You look ghastly!" Shirley's voice interrupted her train of thoughts.

Shirley sat up and stretched luxuriously. "I never thought I could sleep in such a situation! But—what's the matter, Bev?"

"It's close in here," Beverly said, suddenly jumping to her feet. "Suppose you curl up here on the box and try to get some real sleep? I'm going to see if I can get a breath of air on deck."

"We shouldn't separate," Shirley protested.

"I won't stay long," Beverly promised. "You can call me if you want me."

Beverly went toward the two guards. They presented a solid front. It was impossible to pass.

"Do either of you speak English?" she demanded.

One shook his head. The other murmured in a guttural voice:

"Speak English."

"I want to go on deck for some air," she said.

The two conferred in Chinese. Then one stepped aside and allowed her to pass. When she went on deck he followed while the other stayed with Shirley.

Beverly went to the rail and leaned over the water. There was a cool night wind and it ruffled her hair. Unpleasant odors drifted up from the muddy water. She noticed neither of them. In the far distance were two twinkling lights that might be the fading yacht or a house on the shore. She did not know which, but she longed to be there.

The boat rocked unsteadily under her feet as a gust of wind billowed the sail. At the wheel, the full length of the boat from where she was, stood two more of the pirates. They talked in low voices. Reflected on the water was the gleam of lamplight pouring from one of the portholes. That must be where the rest of the murderous crew were, talking and laughing over their hideous success. Probably planning what they would do with the two Americans thrust so opportunely into their hands.

Somehow, right at that moment, it did not seem to matter very much what they did. Tomorrow she would feel differently, would live in dread of the time when the pirate captain should acquaint them with his plans. But now she felt as if her whole world had suddenly gone topsy-turvy. She had to get used to thinking of Shirley with Jim.

Somehow she had always thought Shirley would someday marry Roger. It had seemed the logical conclusion. They were both rich, both held prominent positions in New York society, and had known each other since childhood. She, Beverly, had even refused some of Roger's invitations to fun and frolic in order to throw him and Shirley more together. But it seemed her matchmaking abilities were misdirected. She had never for one instant suspected Shirley of being anything but good friends with Jim. Even now, she might be wrong. Shirley might love him only as a gay comrade, as all of the "Susabella" passengers cared for each other. But that she doubted. There had seemed to be something intangible, something deep and unexplainable, in Shirley's tone when she dreamed about Jim.

Beverly surveyed the little, creaking ship with dark, troubled eyes. Yes, now she thought of it, she could remember Shirley's exact words that night in Cairo. It had been their last night in the historical city and they had stood on the balcony of their room. Shirley had said then:

" 'Beverly—is it Jim?—or Roger? It means a lot to you—as well as to me.' "

Beverly told herself she should have guessed then. Shirley had practically told her!

With a sigh she turned back to her contemplation of the water. She could do nothing now—if indeed there was anything to be done! They would have to wait and see what happened while they were with the pirates, and what happened when and if they were returned to their friends. Somehow the

"Susabella" seemed particularly far away right now.

"Beverly Gray! You get into more trouble than any six people in the United States!" a voice declared dryly.

Beverly looked around sharply. There was no one in sight—that is, no one but the Chinese guard leaning nonchalantly upon his rifle scarcely three feet away.

Strange, she thought. The voice had seemed familiar. She was hearing all sorts of things tonight——

"Yes, sir! Little Miss Dynamite, herself. That's you."

This was no trick of her imagination. There was a voice speaking to her! A familiar, laughter-haunted American voice. But as yet she could not place it so she remained silent. Where did it come from? The water under her feet? Impossible! The cabin behind her where she had left Shirley? That was equally absurd because the two guards were between her and the door. The guards were——

"If you are worrying about Jim—don't. He will be all right in a week or so."

"Larry Owens!" she gasped, turning about and facing the guide who had informed her "Speak English!" and followed her on deck. "Come out from behind that false face."

"It isn't a false face," he contradicted. "Merely grease paint and a little dirt. In fact," he grinned, "more than a little dirt. I haven't seen a bathtub in three weeks."

"What are you doing here—like this?" she demanded.

"I'm a pirate," he answered nonchalantly.

"Seriously!" she said.

"Careful," he warned. He edged a little nearer. "I'm a pirate. I always did want to be a pirate and kidnap beautiful young ladies."

"You weren't responsible for the raid on the 'Susabella'," she murmured. "What is this all about—this masquerade?"

"I'm seeing China at firsthand," he told her smilingly.

Beverly turned and stared out over the water.

"Are you still tracing the man you told me about in India?"

"Yes."

"This is the last place I expected to see anyone I knew, but I'm glad," she whispered.

"You mustn't worry," he said. "I'll try to help you all I can."

"Where are they taking us?"

"There's a little village down the river where they have a hide-out. They will probably stay there until they receive the money they want from your friends."

"How long will that be?" she asked.

"I can't say. It depends on Roger and the rest."

Larry's presence did lend her added confidence but she realized that since he was here in disguise, his own position so precarious, that he could do little

to aid them without exposing his real identity and
involving them all in further danger. Still, nothing
really serious could happen to them if Larry were
present.

"You must not tell Shirley who I am," he said.
"Everyone who knows makes it all the more dangerous. I shouldn't have told you but——"

"I'm glad," she whispered. "It won't be so hard
now. You'll be near——"

"I'll try to get the job of being your steady guard,"
he said. "Not a bad job," he declared with a grin.
"One good thing is that most of these men don't
speak or understand English."

"But how did you ever join up with this crew?"
she wanted to know.

It never would have occurred to anyone watching
the two that such a conversation was being carried
on. Beverly was staring out over the water. Larry,
in his disreputable pirate clothes, leaned on his rifle
and stared at the deck. His face was perfectly im-
movable. Only the barest movement of his lips was
visible to a close observer.

"Oh, I knew a man that knew a man that knew a
man——" he said lightly. "First thing I knew I had
joined up with this fellow because I could shoot the
top off a candle at twenty-five paces."

"But why?" Beverly asked. "Is the man you're
after a pirate?"

"No," Larry said. "He isn't a pirate. In fact, I've
heard that he is very much of a gentleman. But he

is tied up somehow with these fellows. The man at the head of the whole shebang is Barney something or other——"

"Barney!" Beverly almost slipped into the water. "Was his name—Black Barney?"

"That's it," Larry nodded. "He has a finger in all sorts of enterprises, runs a gambling den at Shanghai, bosses the river pirates, promotes revolutions—oh, a likable chap."

"What does he look like?" Beverly asked, gripping the rail tightly.

"Like a gorilla," Larry said promptly, "only uglier. If he ever looked in a mirror he would scare himself. I don't think he will be at this river hideaway, still——"

"You are hoping he will," Beverly said.

"I'd like to meet him," Larry acknowledged.

Beverly felt that it was a queer stroke of fate to bring them to Black Barney at this time. He was the one man in the Orient whom they should have been anxious to avoid. He had half of Slim's map and Jim had the other half. Since the Count was working for Barney she had a fair idea of what would happen if Barney should come to know who they were. Perhaps he already knew and that was why she and Shirley had been taken from the "Susabella." Perhaps the price asked for their return would be Jim's map! She hadn't thought of that before. It would be the best possible way for Barney to secure it. She was sure her friends would give him anything he asked.

"Of all the people in China it would be Black Barney whom we would meet," she laughed in a harsh voice.

"How do you know him?" Larry asked suspiciously. "I didn't know you had such friends."

"Friend!" Beverly exclaimed. Rapidly she told him of the map and the peculiar circumstances surrounding it. She sketched very briefly every contact they had had with the Count.

"Why didn't you tell me this before?" he demanded. "It's no end exciting! Is it a buried treasure or something?"

"We haven't the faintest idea," she said. "The map makes absolutely no sense at all without the other half, and I suppose the other isn't any good without our piece."

"Oh, ho!" Larry exclaimed. "If Barney knows you are two of the ones blocking his chances at a hidden fortune——" His voice trailed away expressively.

"Not a very pleasant thought, is it?" she asked dryly.

"You would never have a chance of getting away then," he said seriously.

"That's what I'm afraid of," Beverly said.

"Has he ever seen you?"

"Not that I know of," she replied.

"That is your one chance then," he said rapidly. "He mustn't find out! Oh, oh! Here comes the big chief. Better go into the cabin," Larry advised.

Beverly turned from her contemplation of the

river and, without a glance in Larry's direction, went down into the smoky cabin to Shirley.

Shirley was curled up on their overturned packing box but she was not asleep. She sat up at Beverly's entrance.

"I thought you might have fallen overboard," she said with a sigh of relief.

Beverly laughed. "The water is too dirty to swim in. Besides, I couldn't even see the shore."

"Bev, how long do you think we'll be here?" Shirley asked with a frightened, distasteful glance around.

"I'm afraid we are here for a long while," Beverly said. "If not actually on the boat, at least in the hands of the pirates."

"Not a chance of escape?" Shirley whispered.

Beverly shook her head. "Not a chance."

"But, Bev, we can't just stay here," Shirley said, horrified. "We don't know what the pirates might do. We saw what happened to J-Jim——"

Beverly put an arm about Shirley. "Don't think about it," she counseled. "We can't help in any way by worrying——"

"But where are we going? What are they going to do?" Shirley persisted.

"We will probably be taken to a camp somewhere along the shore," Beverly said, "and held until Roger or Jim or someone sends the money for our release."

"Roger and Jim will come after us," Shirley said confidently. "Jim will come, I know it!"

"Jim will come," Beverly agreed gravely.

"If he can," Shirley corrected herself, remembering suddenly. "Oh, Bev, do you suppose——"

"Hush," Beverly admonished. "We said we would not think about it any more. We should get what rest we can now. We don't know what might come tomorrow."

"Tomorrow," Shirley agreed thoughtfully.

The thought of the day to come was not pleasant. They had no happy anticipation for what would happen. Tomorrow would bring the pirates and their plans into action. The pirate chief might be busy now with other details of his business, too busy to pay much attention to his captives. But on the morrow he would recall them and what would happen then they could not suppose.

It was a little comforting to Beverly to know that Larry was near. Though what possible aid he could give them she did not know. Any false move he might make would only reveal his identity and then all the work he had done so far would go for naught. His secret mission did not lend itself favorably to rescuing maidens in distress. If he should reveal himself now in his true colors he would have no hope of catching the man he was after.

Another thought cheered her a little. If they were in reality being taken to Black Barney perhaps they could hope for a little better treatment than if they were left solely in the hands of Chinese. Blackguard though the man might be he was an American, a native countryman of theirs. Surely that should mean something to him! She really should not hope for much in that direction. If he was as ruthless and as daring as Larry had intimated, they could expect no measure of consideration!

"Of what are you thinking?" Shirley asked suddenly.

"Of our predicament," Beverly smiled. "We are the unluckiest two girls in the world, I believe."

"For anyone who likes excitement those are traitorous words," Shirley said. "I'll wager Lenora is wishing she were here."

Lenora was, at that very moment, bewailing her fate of being left behind. Whether sincerely or not, she declared her willingness to change places with either Beverly or Shirley.

"If you don't stop chattering so much," Lois said wrathfully, "we'll wish the pirates *had* taken you!"

The lounge was the gathering place for a rather gloomy set of young people. Miss Ernwood, though pale and with a worried frown on her face, seemed the most self-possessed. Roger and Jim, the latter with his arm in a sling and a bulge of bandage under the shoulder of his coat, paced the floor tirelessly. Lois and Lenora tried to sit calmly but were not very successful.

"Where do you suppose they've taken them?" Lenora murmured for the tenth time.

Paul and Terry entered the lounge.

"The radio is in working order again," Terry informed the group. "And the Captain is making full steam for Canton."

"What can the police do?" Roger said helplessly.

"They've never been able to catch river pirates," Jim said gloomily.

"We didn't have a chance against them," Paul continued. "They seemed to come from out of nowhere."

"Do you suppose they'll demand a ransom?" Lenora asked, wide-eyed.

"Certainly," Lois said. "Pirates always do."

"All this talk isn't getting us anywhere," Jim said desperately. "Can't we *do* something?"

"You should go to bed," Lenora said bluntly. "With that shoulder——"

"I couldn't sleep." Jim waved the suggestion aside. "If we could only go after them——"

Roger stopped in his stride and stared at them. He snapped his fingers suddenly. "I think I've got it!"

"Don't let it get away from you," Lenora begged. "What is it?"

"Woo!" Roger yelled. "Woo Fong! Woo—come here!"

"Yessa, yessa." The Chinese cook came from the kitchen, bowing.

"Woo, I want you to do something for me," Roger said. "Something important!"

Woo inclined his head. "Impoltant! Yessa!"

"When those fellows boarded our boat a while

ago, Woo, you saw them. You saw all of them. Think, think carefully! Did you know any of them? Tell the truth, Woo! I want the truth or, by the beards of all your ancestors, I'll throw you overboard!"

Woo faced his young master. The tense, white look on Roger's face lent insistence to his words. Slowly the cook looked from one to the other of the rigid and intent group.

"The bones of all your ancestors will turn over in their graves if you lie, Woo," Terry put in, leaning close to the Chinaman. "You will lose the regard of your countrymen if you lie to the master who has been faithful to you all these years."

Woo nodded. "Woo Fong tell tluth. I—I know but one of the unspeakable pigs!"

"The name pig just suits them," Lenora declared.

"Shshshsh," Lois cautioned.

"In Shanghai and Canton Woo play fan-tan," the cook said slowly.

"Fan-tan is a Chinese game played in the gambling houses," Lenora explained unnecessarily to Lois.

Lois gave her an exasperated glance and turned her attention to Roger and his servant.

"Did you lose your money to one of them?" Roger asked with a smile.

Woo Fong's head bobbed up and down emphatically.

"It is so. To the unworthy dog with the scar——"

"Such complimentary names," Lenora murmured.

"Woo, do you know where the pirates have gone?"

"I am not shuah——"

"He isn't sure!" Lenora said excitedly. "But he might know!"

"If you aren't still we'll throw you overboard," Lois threatened.

"Could you take us there?" Roger asked intently.

Woo Fong looked about again at the anxious faces. He shook his head.

"Woo Fong is not shuah——"

"But you think you know where they've gone!" Roger said firmly. "I know you have been away from China for a long while, Woo—many years. But you know the people—you have friends here—you speak the language."

"Woo Fong has been away many yeah——"

"Many years," Roger agreed. He leaned a little closer. "If you want to go back with us, Woo, you will do as I ask you now."

Woo Fong inclined his head dutifully.

"Woo has fliends but many changes have come to Woo's countly——"

"Hang the changes!" Roger shouted. "Woo, can you find those pirates?"

"Alone—mebbe," Woo shrugged. His eyes were shining in the yellow lamplight. "Woo lived many yeahs along the rice fields——"

"Along here?" Jim put in. "Find those pirates, Woo, help us rescue Miss Gray and Miss Parker, and you will be the biggest hero in all China! You can have anything in the world you want."

"Can have holiday?" Woo grinned.

"As long as you want," Roger promised.

"Woo go now." The cook bowed and turned to the corridor.

"Wait a minute!" Roger was after him. "Where are you going? We're headed for Canton."

"No go to Canton." Woo shook his head. "Put little boat down. Woo pull to land."

"Do you want any money or—or anything?" Terry put in.

"But can't you tell us where you are going? Where will we see you?" Roger insisted. "Where can the boat wait for you?"

Woo shrugged. "Anyplace. Woo not care."

"Is there a harbor anywhere along the shore?" Paul questioned.

Woo shook his head. "Best go to Canton."

"We'll not go to Canton!" Jim declared positively. "That is miles away! We want to be at hand if any-thing—— When the girls are returned."

"We will anchor close to this spot," Roger in-formed Woo. "We will wait four days. Then we will go to Canton for police and return. We will find the pirates if we have to search every foot along the riverbank!"

Woo bowed, his face perfectly expressionless. "Me go now."

Paul and Roger went up on deck to help Woo lower a small rowboat into the water. They watched, straining their eyes through the darkness as scarcely a ripple disturbed the water where the oars rested.

The engine of the "Susabella" slowed the rhythmic pounding. The boat floated gently on the swell of the river.

"Do you think we can trust Woo?" Lois murmured wonderingly when they were all together again.

"Do you think he will turn against his own countrymen?" added Lenora.

"You've heard the saying 'set a thief to catch a thief'," Paul contributed.

"But this is different," argued Lenora. "After all, he might have been in league with the pirates. Perhaps Woo Fong told them just where the yacht would be and when to catch us unawares."

Roger shook his head. "I think Woo will be faithful to me. We've got to put our trust in him. It is our only chance!"

"One of us should have gone with him," Jim frowned.

"We wouldn't have had a chance," Terry argued. "This fellow speaks their language. He knows how to treat his fellows. A white man would never have found a band of Chinese who wanted to remain hidden."

"I suppose you're right," Jim sighed heavily.

"Yet it is hard," Lois declared, "to know that perhaps Beverly's and Shirley's—lives depend on our cook!"

All through the night their minds were troubled

with the wonder of Woo Fong's faithfulness. Were they right in putting so much absolute trust and faith in the little Chinese? Would Roger's promise of a "holiday" be sufficient to hold him faithful to their cause?

With the first gray streaks of dawn the yacht drew as close as possible to the shore and dropped anchor. At least they could remain this close to the scene of their misfortune.

CHAPTER XIII

The Villain

EARLY IN THE MORNING the pirate junk anchored along the riverbank. To give the scattering of huts the name of village was flattering it far too much. The girls were escorted to a small, brown hovel nestling close to the earth a little apart from the others. Through the group of houses ran a trail of wagon ruts and over this road sometimes, as when the girls first saw it, mules pulled jolting carts.

Beverly and Shirley exchanged dismayed glances when they first viewed the pirate stronghold. It was a scene of desolation. Muddy fields stretched away into a hillside covered with a growth of bamboo. Not a white face was visible. From the huts cautious faces peeked out as the girls were marched to the hut assigned to them.

Beverly had managed to place herself beside Larry and as they walked she asked him questions. He answered, assuming the necessary unwillingness for his pirate role.

"Who's hut is that?" she wanted to know, indicating by far the largest house with its matted roof and paper windowpanes. The other buildings as far as she could see had no window covering at all.

"The chief's place," Larry said, "or so they tell me. You are to stay here." He stepped aside and let Shirley and Beverly precede him into a dark, earthen room. "I'll see what I can do about some breakfast for you."

"Who is he?" Shirley whispered to Beverly. "Seems anxious about us—for one of the pirate gang."

"Evidently the only one who speaks English," Beverly said, frowning. "What a place this is!" Purposely she changed the subject. Larry had asked her not to reveal his identity to Shirley on the principle that each one who knew increased the possibility of his being discovered. Though, Beverly reflected, when he spoke to her so solicitously, Shirley could not help but wonder.

"Are we supposed to sleep standing up?" Shirley demanded.

Beverly had discovered a candle but there were no matches with which to light it. The single window and open doorway did not afford much light in the early dawn. When the sun was up she supposed it would be better.

They discovered a couple of straw mats flung into the corner.

"I refuse to sleep on them," Shirley said positively. "I'll lean against the wall first."

"I don't blame you," Beverly said. "We'll have to do something about this. If they expect to get a million dollars"—she laughed over the amount—"they should at least make us comfortable."

One soapbox and a rickety table completed the furnishings. Shirley regarded it all ruefully.

"We'll have to take turns sitting on the box," she said with a flash of humor.

"You sit on the box and I'll sit on the table," Beverly proposed, hoisting herself upon it.

Her energy proved her undoing. The table, long unused to such use, collapsed beneath her and Beverly found herself sitting on the earthen floor amid a pile of splinters. She looked up at Shirley and both burst into laughter.

The laughter did much to lighten their spirits.

" 'Humpty Dumpty sat on a wall,' " Shirley quoted with a giggle.

"Only in this case it was a table," Beverly agreed, getting laboriously to her feet. "And I am still here."

"For which three cheers," Shirley said fervently. "I should hate to be here by myself!"

Beverly shivered. "I hadn't thought of that, but it would be pretty awful if one were alone. We can be each other's moral support."

There was a noise outside and Larry entered, bearing two bowls of rice and two pairs of chopsticks.

"Do we have to eat with those things?" Shirley demanded.

"You can use your fingers if you like," Beverly laughed. "I wish we had practiced as Lois and Lenora did."

Larry went out again without a word. A cautious peek out the door disclosed the fact that a guard was sitting cross-legged on the ground, his rifle within easy reach. Beverly's heart sank, because the man wasn't Larry.

The solitary street was deserted. Occasionally a sign of life stirred within the other brown huts. Off-shore the junk rode at anchor, swaying with the swell of the water.

With a deep sigh Shirley, at Beverly's insistence, spread one of the straw mats over the box and sat down, balancing her bowl of rice precariously on her knee while she juggled the chopsticks. Beverly watched her with a smile.

"How is it going?"

"The rice is awful," Shirley answered, her mouth full. "Do you suppose we shall have to eat this for every meal?"

"We might get dried fish once in a while," Beverly said.

"That would be a treat," Shirley murmured with a wry face. "Just think of Woo Fong's delicious dinners on the 'Susabella' as compared to this."

The hours ticked slowly past. The girls stared moodily out the window or paced the small confines of their room.

"If something doesn't happen soon I'll scream!"

Shirley declared viciously as the sun sank beneath the horizon.

Beverly could sympathize with her friend. This inactivity was nerve-racking, but to her own way of thinking, any delay was hopeful. As long as Black Barney had not sent for them so far perhaps the man was not here. If he were not, then he could not know that the two captives were members of the party who held the much-sought-after map. No news was good news she believed. Also, a delay might mean action on the part of the "Susabella." She could not believe that their friends would sit calmly by and do nothing. Jim, if he were able, would be sure to start a search for—Shirley. Jim and Shirley! Jim and Shirley! The two names repeated themselves over and over in her mind. Restlessly, she turned from the window and walked to the door.

She stood there, looking out as the world grew dark with night. The guard watched her closely. Shirley came and put an arm within Beverly's.

"I wish we could make a dash for it," she said wistfully.

"Where would we run?" Beverly countered. "We don't know the country—we couldn't hope to man their boat alone——"

"Here comes someone," Shirley whispered excitedly.

A lone figure was making his way from the largest of the huts, behind the paper windowpanes of which flickered occasional shadows.

"It looks as though your wish for action was about to be fulfilled," Beverly agreed.

The figure, clothes baggy and misshapen, dissolved out of the darkness into the dirtiest of the lot of Chinese. Shirley mistrusted his streaked, dirty face, yet at the same time the set of his head, the stride of his long legs, struck a faintly reminiscent chord in her memory.

Beverly recognized Larry and felt a sense of relief. At least he was still among those present.

Larry consulted briefly with the guard. Then he turned to Beverly.

"Follow!" he said and marched away.

"Isn't he gruesome," Shirley chattered as she and Beverly fell into step behind Larry. "I think he is the evilest-looking one of the lot."

Beverly smiled. "Mmmmm," she agreed.

It did not take long to walk to the hut of the chief. The ground was full of ruts and the girls stumbled frequently, yet Larry did not slacken his rapid gait.

"What's the rush?" Shirley demanded fretfully. "Whoever it is can wait until we get there!" She halted and ruefully rubbed an ankle which had come in contact with a stone.

"Shirley!" Beverly whispered hastily. "Look!" Beverly indicated the corner of one building.

At first Shirley thought she meant to dash around it and try to elude the pirates. But gradually her eyes picked out of the dusk a small, husky figure standing there. As they neared the building she thought she recognized the figure. Suddenly she stopped in her tracks and clutched Beverly's arm tightly.

"Bev! I see him! Is it Woo Fong?"

"If it isn't, it is his twin brother," Beverly murmured. "What is he doing here?"

"Do you suppose the 'Susabella'——" Shirley began. She turned and looked toward the river. But no comforting hulk loomed out of the blackness. Only the junk was anchored there, in solitary state.

Puzzled by the sight of the familiar figure the girls went on more slowly after Larry. They stepped into a room much similar to the one they had left only with more furnishings. There were chairs and a table upon which stood two flickering candles. Behind the table sat a man, a white man. Two Chinamen stood against the wall, one cleaning a rifle.

Instinctively, Beverly knew the man sitting behind the table was Black Barney. He was a huge person, easily over six feet in height when he rose, as he did now, to confront them. His hair and eyes were black as coal. His skin was tanned as deeply as a Malaga's. His face was lined and cruel. Beverly knew they could expect no consideration from him and her heart sank, but she did not propose to let him know she was in the least afraid.

The two girls stood silently before him, viewing him with the same curiosity that he regarded them. There were steps behind them and the man who had captained the boat entered. He spoke rapidly to

Barney in Chinese. Once he glanced toward Beverly and rubbed his cheek reflectively. Beverly supposed he was telling his chief how she slapped his face when he attempted to take her bracelet from her. No matter what came from the event, she was not sorry she had done it.

"Hi, yaaaa!" A high, piping voice intoned pleadingly.

Into the hut swept an outraged pirate, dragging behind him a protesting, wriggling, wailing Woo Fong.

Shirley gripped Beverly's hand tightly. She had been hoping Woo Fong was there to help them. Now it seemed he was in the same predicament they were.

"Who's this?" Barney demanded wrathfully.

The pirate gestured wildly as he chattered away in his high singsong voice.

"Allee same velly solly," Woo Fong interposed at the end.

"So you speak English!" Barney said in surprise. "What were you doing hiding in my camp? What do you want here? Speak up!"

"Want join pilates," Woo Fong grinned.

"Fool!" Barney declared. "Do you expect me to believe that?"

Woo shrugged his shoulders. "Lose money to Chin Chang. Must join pilates to get money."

"Chin, is that right? Did you take his money?" One of the other Chinamen nodded.

"Have you ever seen either of these two girls before?" Barney demanded of Woo, shoving the little man over before the girls.

Woo squinted at them closely, finally shaking his head.

"No see befoah."

Beverly squeezed Shirley's fingers to keep her friend silent. As it was, she was afraid Barney had noticed the dismay and astonishment on the other girl's features.

The man called Chin stepped forward and whispered to Barney.

"Never seen them before, eh?" Barney said viciously. "Dog! You are from the same boat. Cook, weren't you?"

"Me velly good cook," Woo Fong agreed. "Me want to join pilates. Aflaid you say no if I come flom boat."

"Are you sure you weren't sent here?" Barney asked. One long arm shot out and gripped Woo Fong by the throat. "If you lie to me——"

"Tell tluth!" Woo assured him fervently.

"Like pilates velly much!" the little man continued. "Me velly fine cook——"

Barney considered it for a moment. "All right," he said, flinging the yellow man away from him. "You'll cook for us. Chin, take him out. I'll talk to him more later."

The hut emptied of all but Beverly, Shirley, Barney, and Larry. The other Chinamen all followed out the newest addition to their group. Their voices echoed back to the four in the little room, gradually dying away in the distance.

Barney sat down behind the table and pushed a piece of paper across at Beverly.

"Sign that," he said tersely.

Beverly picked up the paper and Shirley read it with her. It was a demand for money and addressed to their friends. If twenty thousand dollars was deposited in a spot, to be arranged later, the girls would be released.

"Twenty thousand dollars is a lot of money," Beverly said, laying the paper back upon the table.

"It should be worth it to them," he said. "Ten thousand for each of you."

"They don't have that much," Shirley said.

"They can get it," he said complacently. "I happen to know the people on board that yacht are rich Americans."

"Not that rich," Beverly said steadily. "Suppose they can't pay it?"

"Then I'm afraid you will become permanent fixtures around here," he laughed dryly. "Sign it." A stub of a pencil was thrown at her.

"What assurance do we have that you will let us go even if they do pay the money?" Beverly asked calmly.

He grinned. "None. But you better sign it. There are ways and means to make you——"

"S-sign it, Bev," Shirley whispered tremulously in her friend's ear.

Beverly shrugged and wrote her name on the slip of paper. Shirley did likewise.

"Now," Beverly said, and there was a glint of recklessness in her eyes, "since you are going to get so much money for us, you should make our stay a little more pleasant."

"This isn't any hotel," he retorted.

"We would like boxes or something to sit on," she went on, sublimely unconscious of his glare. "A table, candles, and decent food. We aren't Chinamen and don't intend to live on rice."

"Spunky, aren't you?" Barney laughed. Beverly's confident manner seemed to delight his sense of humor.

"Lu Wing, get some candles," he ordered Larry curtly.

Larry bowed and went out. He returned in scarcely a second, with two candles in his hand. He lighted them from the candles on the table and held them, fostering the small flame.

"We'll see what else we can do," Barney told Beverly, rising and coming around the table.

Beverly watched him suspiciously. There was something wrong. No pirate chief should take orders from his prisoners—at least, not so good naturedly or meekly.

"You're the one slapped Min Lung's face, aren't you?" Barney grinned.

Beverly nodded speechlessly and backed away a little, instinctively moving closer to Larry.

"As long as you are here for a while we should become friends," Barney continued. His hand closed suddenly on Beverly's arm. "Come here."

Larry had been shielding the candle flames from the air that circulated in the room, keeping their feeble spark of life burning. The wax melted and ran down the side. Now, with scarcely a movement, he held the candles so the hot wax dropped on Barney's hand.

"Clumsy fool!" Barney roared, releasing Beverly automatically. He aimed a kick at Larry but the latter side-stepped.

"Velly solly," Larry murmured meekly. "Did not know wax was hot. Velly solly," he repeated.

"Get out!" Barney said viciously, wiping the wax from his hand. "And take these two back to their hut. I'll see them later."

The girls were glad enough to escape from their captor.

"Do you suppose it was an accident or did he drop the wax on that man on purpose?" Shirley whispered to Beverly as they walked before Larry back to their black hut.

Beverly thought it had been on purpose but she did not say so. At the moment of the happening her heart had been in her throat. What had been Barney's intentions? She could not have done anything right then. Only Larry's quick action had aided them. As it was, she was afraid it was only a temporary respite.

If the people on board the "Susabella" did not do

something quickly, if they could not pay the amount of money——

"Do you suppose Roger can get the money?" Shirley whispered as they entered the hut.

"It is a huge sum," Beverly frowned. "Where will they get it?"

Larry put the candles into grooves in the mud walls and left them alone.

"Lenora has a fortune; she could help," Shirley said ponderously.

"Leave it to us to get into a mess like this," Beverly said, pacing the floor. "We can't expect them to pay all that money. It is a fortune in itself."

"If they don't——" Shirley's voice broke. "What'll we do, Bev?"

Beverly sighed, running her fingers through her curly hair. "I wish I knew! I'd do it now."

"What do you think about Woo Fong?" Shirley continued. "Deserting us! Saying he never saw us before! If Roger knew, he would——"

Two men entered carrying low army cots. Beverly and Shirley exchanged glances. The former could not restrain a smile. Barney was evidently willing to give them the minor comforts.

"I am astonished!" Shirley declared, seating herself on one of them. "I thought we would have to sleep on the floor."

"I am astonished that he did what I asked him," Beverly grinned. A moment later she became serious. "I wonder what——"

"What?" Shirley asked.

"Oh, nothing," Beverly evaded.

She had been going to say she wondered why Barney was doing these things. Perhaps he would tack an added thousand or so onto the demand he was sending to the "Susabella."

How would they ever get away from this place? The more she thought about it, the more she sought for a means of escape, the more hopeless it seemed. Larry had promised to aid them but he had his own work to consider. Too, she had no idea when he would decide to come to their rescue. Perhaps they could not wait that long. There had been something in Barney's tone tonight she did not like.

Had he discovered that the people on the "Susabella" were the ones who had the map? It was her belief that Shirley's, and her own, safety depended upon that fact.

The girls slept but fitfully that night. The strangeness, the silence, of the place disturbed them. They were afraid of something unseen, something inexplainable, yet felt in the very air. It was as if a sword were hanging over their heads and threatened at any moment to fall.

"I don't want another night like that," Shirley declared positively. "I didn't close my eyes all night!"

There was more rice for breakfast and hot tea. For lunch they had rice cakes and dried fish.

Shirley threw the bowl onto the floor viciously.

"I won't eat it!" she said positively. "I'll starve first!"

"You might at that," Beverly said wryly. "If Woo is cooking for them he must have left his cookbook on board the 'Susabella'."

"Where do you suppose they are?" Shirley asked dreamily. "Do you suppose they've got the letter yet?"

"I can't say," Beverly said. She was staring out the window.

"What are you looking at?" Shirley demanded.

"Come here," Beverly invited. "Look!"

There was a sudden uproar outside. Two carts pulled by patient donkeys had halted before the larger hut. From the first cart crawled a white man. He took off his hat and stood looking around him. Beverly drew Shirley back from the window so that they could see but not be seen.

"Recognize him?" Beverly asked anxiously. "Count Alexis!"

"*What?* Are you sure?" Shirley demanded.

Beverly was sure. There was no mistaking the man who stood in the bright sunlight and viewed the scene about him. Evidently the desolation was as appalling to him as it had been to them.

What was he doing here? That was Beverly's worry. Now there was no chance of keeping their identity a secret from Barney. He would know where the map was once he talked to the Count. Too, she was sure they had small chance of escaping now. The Count would be more than anxious to keep them there until the map had been procured.

"That rather narrows our chances, doesn't it?" Shirley murmured, regarding her friend with worried eyes.

"It does," Beverly agreed. She watched the Count disappear into the hut where they had met Black Barney. And to think she had once believed the Count when he said Barney was no friend of his! To think she had once been friends with Count Alexis! It made her angry every time she thought of it.

"Well?" Shirley continued.

"Well what?" she asked irritatedly.

"What is going to happen now?" Shirley wanted to know.

"Fireworks!" Beverly said briefly. "I'd like to be a long way off when Black Barney finds out who we are."

"Black Barney!" Shirley echoed. "You mean—you mean that man is the one who has the other half of our map?"

Beverly nodded.

"How do you know?" Shirley said breathlessly. "I mean, perhaps he isn't——"

"He is," Beverly said. "I can't tell you how I know but I do."

"If Jim or Roger would only come!" Shirley whispered. "If they would only do something."

"Yes," Beverly said, turning away. "If Jim would only do something."

"Do you think they went back to Canton?"

"I suppose so," Beverly said, sitting down upon her bed.

"What's wrong, Bev?" Shirley asked, crossing and seating herself beside her chum.

"What do you mean?"

"What is the matter with you? Are you only worried about our predicament or is it—something else? You've seemed different ever since the pirates got hold of us." She put an arm about Beverly. "Tell a pal," she said anxiously. "Or—or have I done something?"

Beverly regarded the tip of her shoe. "No," she said, "you haven't done anything."

"Then what——"

"Shirley"—Beverly turned to her suddenly—"do —do you lo——" She turned away abruptly. "Forget it. It isn't anything."

Shirley turned worried eyes upon her. "I wish you would tell me——"

Beverly went to the window and stood staring out. A sudden noise beneath the window attracted her attention. A man was sitting cross-legged on the ground, industriously cleaning a rifle. She recognized the broad shoulders, ineffectively disguised beneath the cotton blouse.

"Beverly——"

"Yes," she breathed.

"Tonight——" The voice continued in a low murmur. "I'm to be the guard at your door. About midnight if all goes well——"

"We'll be ready," Beverly promised in a low voice.

Larry got to his feet, inspected the rifle, and, as if satisfied with his work, shambled away.

There was a happy gleam in Beverly's eyes as she turned back to Shirley.

"What was it?" Shirley wanted to know.

"Nothing," Beverly said swiftly. Then as the glow faded from Shirley's face she continued: "But I shouldn't be surprised if we get some action tonight."

"Do you know something you haven't told me?" Shirley demanded.

Beverly nodded. "I can't tell you though I'd like to. But, perhaps, tonight——"

"Oh, I'm so happy at the thought of leaving this place." Shirley hugged her chum expressively. Beverly did not return the friendly embrace very fervently and Shirley was hurt though she did not show it. She could not imagine what was wrong with Beverly. Sometimes she caught Beverly looking at her with a queer, contemplative look in her eyes that Shirley could not fathom. It must be the emergency in which they found themselves. Now, hope of rescue chased everything else from Shirley's thoughts. She had a million questions to ask Beverly but she doubted if her chum would answer them.

The rest of the afternoon dragged interminably. Beverly was afraid that any moment Barney might bring the Count to them. She was afraid of what might happen if they were brought face to face with the man they had eluded so long. She even reflected grimly that she might slap his face as she had the pirate captain's. That would do her no good, she knew. But it would help to let out the forces of pent-up energy, anger, and impotence that raged in her heart.

At nightfall Larry duly exchanged places with the guard at their door. Barney had no cause so far to suspect him so he trusted the two girls to his care.

Beverly could not repress a sense of delight when they were alone with only Larry between them and freedom. She stood in the doorway and they talked guardedly, in the barest of whispers.

"There's a good wind tonight," Larry was saying. "If we can get aboard their junk, cut it loose, and hoist the sail the breeze will carry us down the river. It is our only chance. We wouldn't have a chance on the land."

"We'll try anything," Beverly said desperately. "But what of your work——"

"I've found out what I came for," Larry replied. "I have to go to Shanghai now."

"Where is Woo Fong?" Beverly wanted to know. "I can't understand his joining up with the pirates. I always thought he was devoted to Roger."

"He is cooking for Barney," Larry chuckled. "I sometimes think he would like to put poison in the tea."

A man appeared in the open carrying two bowls and he came toward the hut. Beverly hastily disappeared inside. There must be no connection between her and the guard.

When the man brought the bowls in, set them down and departed, Shirley looked at them disgustedly.

"Don't tell me what it is. Let me guess," she proposed with a twinkle. "Could it be waffles or ice cream?"

"Both," Beverly laughed. "Chinese waffles and ice cream."

There was a sauce on the dried fish that did increase its savoriness. They attributed this to Woo Fong's cooking ability.

After their dinner they tried to rest a while. It was near midnight when Beverly got up and in the darkness approached the door. They had not lighted the candles so there was no flicker to give evidence of any movement within the hovel. Behind her, Shirley noiselessly followed.

"Is it time?" Beverly whispered to Larry.

He came from the shadows close to the wall. For a few seconds he looked about. Only the faint light from the stars illumined the site. Beyond, at the river, the junk still rode at anchor. Not a soul was stirring. There was no sign of life anywhere.

"It is time," Larry agreed. "Follow me and make no noise!"

"Who is he?" Shirley whispered as she joined Beverly and the two fell into step behind Larry.

"Larry Owens," Beverly answered briefly. Now that the time had come for their escape there could be no harm in Shirley's knowing.

Shirley's curiosity was running riot but she did not ask questions now. It was not an opportune time for it. She could only be thankful that there was someone for them to depend on. They had much needed help in this hour. Later, when once they were safe, she could ask all the questions she liked. But now silence was essential and they did everything to preserve it.

Cautiously, stepping lightly and carefully so as not to disturb any stones that might make a noise and rouse the men, they made their way past Barney's hut. The junk loomed before them as a well to a man dying of thirst. It was the haven they must reach! They must board it and sail down the river. No other way could they avoid Barney and the Count.

Beverly thought fleetingly of the wrath of the pirates when they found their quarry gone. Once more they would have outwitted the Count, too. But, on the other hand, woe to them if they failed! If they should be discovered now! If Larry's identity were revealed there was no telling what would happen. Barney would be angry enough to murder them all.

"Larry," she whispered as they hurried along, "do you suppose there is a guard on the boat?"

"There was," he grinned down at her. "But I took care of him this afternoon. All we have to do now is reach it and——"

There was a sudden shout. Disaster was upon them. A shot rang out. The bullet whistled past Beverly's ear. Larry drew the girls down to the ground as a volley of shots poured forth as the pirates emerged, seeking the cause of the first explosion.

"We've got to run for it!" Larry said. "I don't think Barney will let them shoot us down but they will try to recapture us. Run, girls!"

Obediently Beverly and Shirley fled, regardless of the noise they made now. Behind them the horde of pirates swooped down. Over her shoulder Beverly caught a glimpse of Woo Fong panting and puffing along in the lead. This was how Woo Fong repaid Roger for all he had done!

Necessity lent wings to their feet. The girls sped over the uneven ground swiftly. Larry followed more slowly, making sure none of the pirates caught up with Beverly or Shirley. But the Chinamen were gaining. There was no doubt of that. Woo Fong was right on Larry's heels. Behind him came Chin Chang.

Black Barney and the Count raced along, the last to join the group. Barney was shouting orders to his men. Suddenly he stopped and aimed a revolver.

"What are you doing?" the Count demanded.

"I'll stop one of them," he said viciously.

"Fool!" Count Alexis exploded, knocking the gun from the other man's hand as Barney pulled the trigger. "You might hit one of the girls and we'd have the police on our necks."

"What difference would it make?" Barney said wrathfully. "If they get to Canton the police will be here anyway."

Beverly and Shirley reached the junk and climbed aboard. Beverly found a knife and with it stood ready to cut the rope that held the anchor. Larry was almost to the boat. He whirled in his tracks and confronted Woo Fong. He was about ready to knock the little Chinaman over when he stopped in surprise. Woo Fong pressed a revolver into Larry's hand.

"Shoot velly fast," Woo Fong counseled and, turning, fired point-blank into the midst of the pirates.

Larry saw Chin stumble and fall. Like lightning his brain comprehended what had happened. Woo Fong was there to help the girls! He laughed suddenly, joyously. A few seconds before he had been almost certain they could not escape. Now they had a very good chance. He leaped for the boat, waved to Beverly, and shouted to Woo Fong. The latter scrambled aboard and Beverly cut the rope.

As if released from enforced captivity the boat jerked away from the pier. Larry and Woo Fong ran and laboriously hoisted the tattered sail.

Beverly and Shirley stood in the stern and watched the group on the shore fade into the night. The darkness soon swallowed up the scene on the shore. They smiled delightedly at one another.

"We made it," Shirley said.

"But we wouldn't have if it hadn't been for Woo Fong," Beverly said. "We certainly misjudged him."

"Woo Fong velly solly not see ladies befoah," Woo Fong spoke behind him. "Mista Logah allee same velly wollied."

"Are they far from here?" Shirley asked eagerly. "Where is the yacht anchored?"

"Someplace along watah," Woo Fong said unsatisfactorily. "Ketchum up pletty soon."

Larry was regarding the sail with dissatisfied eyes.

"We'll make out all right if the wind holds out," he said.

"Do you suppose they have another boat?" Shirley asked anxiously.

"I don't think so," Larry assured her. "But I would like to get as far away as soon as possible."

"Woo Fong, was Mr. Stanton hurt badly?" Shirley was inquiring.

"Mista Stanton alle same fine," Woo Fong assured her.

"Then he wasn't killed!" Shirley sighed.

"Him fine," the Chinaman repeated.

"Did you hear that, Beverly?" Shirley cried.

"Yes," Beverly answered.

"Aren't you glad?" Shirley wanted to know, puzzled with Beverly's seeming indifference.

"Of course I'm glad," Beverly said promptly.

"Larry, do you suppose the junk will take us all the way to Canton?"

Shirley gazed after her friend in surprise as Beverly went with Larry to where they could inspect the sail more minutely. Was Beverly actually so heartless? There had been no spontaneous relief or joy at the news of Jim's escape. Yet Beverly must be relieved! She must be glad! Shirley could not understand her friend. They used to be such good chums, told one another practically everything, yet now every day seemed to set them farther apart. This experience with the pirates should have drawn them closer together, increased their dependence upon one another. Yet Beverly was strangely aloof. Oh, it was nothing that Shirley could definitely point to as an end to their friendship. Beverly was still friendly, still gay and understanding, but there was a difference. She was a friend but with reservations. She was willing to listen to Shirley's difficulties and to help but she did not confide anything of her own in Shirley. That was not Shirley's idea of friendship. She wanted to share just as much of Beverly's difficulties. Shirley was sure there was something troubling Beverly. She had felt that way in Cairo. For weeks she had noticed that Beverly was different, but only since they had been captured by the pirates had it come to the fore so noticeably.

The breeze puffed the sail and the boat progressed rapidly at first. The black water was calm, stirred only as the boat drifted through it. But soon it became apparent that the wind was dying down. The wind lessened and the boat decreased in its speed.

Larry was worried and his uneasiness was reflected in the other three members of the "crew." If the wind stopped, the boat would be helpless. The pirates, if they found another vessel, would have man power with which to come after them. The number of men at the hideaway could easily row a boat and catch up to them as they stood still waiting for the wind to pick up.

"Could we reach the shore, do you suppose?" Shirley asked.

Larry shook his head. "I don't think it would help much. We wouldn't be able to make much progress even then."

An hour before dawn a vague stirring of the water began. Clouds hovered low overhead. Rain pattered on the river. The four took refuge below deck. The storm grew in volume. The boat which had only a short while ago drifted so easily on the water was tossed about now like a toy. The hurricane they had experienced off the coast of India was repeating itself, only now they did not have a sturdy yacht on which to ride it out.

"Perhaps we should have stayed with the pirates a little longer," Shirley said with a wry smile.

"I don't know which is the worse," Beverly agreed. "Do you think we'll stay right side up?" she asked Larry.

He shook his head. "I doubt it."

"Oh, dear," Shirley sighed. "And not a life preserver in sight."

Woo Fong huddled in a corner, his usually smiling face pale and thoughtful. The girls and Larry held onto whatever was firmly secured. It was the only way they could keep from being tossed about with the boat.

"We'll have to go on deck," Larry said finally.

"We don't want to be caught in the cabin when the boat goes down," agreed Beverly.

It was impossible to stand upright on deck without clinging to something for support. Larry found a rope and looped it about each of them, forming a chain that bound them together.

"We won't get lost now if the worst should come," he said steadily. He had discarded much of his Chinese make-up but his skin had still a yellowish tint.

Water was flung in their faces; the wind whipped their clothes about them, drenching them with rain and river water. A sudden gust tore the mast from its moorings and sent it crashing almost on top of the two girls.

Shirley huddled beside Beverly and tried to be as brave as possible. She even managed a smile for Beverly's benefit but she was scared to death. She didn't mind admitting the fact and told Beverly so.

"You're not the only one," Beverly replied. "I hope this is the closest I ever come to seeing Davy Jones's locker."

"What was it Lenora used to say? 'Deep and damp

and dingy and old, Is the grave where the pirates' bones are rolled,' " Shirley quoted through chattering teeth.

"Hush," Beverly said sternly. "It is bad enough without——" Her words died away in a scream.

Quite suddenly the little junk was no longer on the water. The wind hurled it over with fiendish glee. The four lone occupants were quickly submerged in the tide of the muddy water.

Beverly came to the surface with difficulty. Weight on the rope around her waist dragged her under again. On one side of her was Larry and on the other was Shirley. It was on the latter side that the tug was firmer. Beverly dove beneath the surface and came up with her friend. She held Shirley afloat while she looked for Larry. He was supporting Woo Fong and the look on Larry's face in other circumstances would have been comical. He gestured to the Chinese cook and yelled:

"He can't swim!"

Shirley was barely able to help herself. Woo Fong collapsed utterly the moment he hit the water. It was all Beverly and Larry could do to keep the other two abreast of the water.

The experience was one none of them would ever forget. Somehow, after what seemed ages of struggle, they came into shallow water and could wade upon the riverbank. Totally exhausted, they sank down on the solid ground and let the storm rage about them.

Beverly opened her eyes and closed them again. Soon she was wide awake. She took the major part of the situation in at one glance. The storm had gone, the sun was shining, her friends were still asleep on the ground beside her, and bending over her was a Chinaman. The latter wore a long blue grown, a short sleeveless jacket and black satin, narrow-toed shoes.

Beverly's first thought had been that the pirates had caught up with them. But upon glancing around she found no one but this man in sight. He could not be a pirate. His costume was too splendid, too costly.

Beverly reached over and pinched Larry's ankle. Then she endeavored to get to her feet. She was stiff and it was a trying procedure to stand up straight but she managed it.

"How—who——" she began uncertainly.

"I am but the humble owner of this most miserable ground," the Chinaman said with the deference of his countrymen and in perfect English. "I came to inspect the damage of the storm and found your most honorable self——"

Voices had awakened Shirley and Larry. The latter soon bestirred Woo Fong with a poke into his ribs. Woo Fong looked upon the stranger who had awakened them and leaped up to bow profoundly.

"Woo Fong!" the newcomer ejaculated. "By all your reverend ancestors! Why are you here?"

"Kin Yang, most gracious Prior Born," Woo Fong said with all proper respect for one far above him in rank and station, "we were caught in the storm having just escaped from those dogs of——"

Kin Yang inclined his stately head.

"Fortune has smiled upon me in delivering you here. All in my humble house is yours to command."

Larry interposed himself at this place.

"If you could give us food and shelter until we may reach our friends and tell them of our safety our gratitude will be unbounded."

Kin Yang smiled. "Come," he said and turned, leading the way inland from the river. As he went he chatted pleasantly with Larry.

"Americans," he continued, "aren't you? I spent many years in your glorious country."

"I never thought it was especially glorious until now," Shirley whispered to Beverly. "But what I wouldn't give to see New York now——"

Beverly nodded in agreement. She, too, was experiencing a heavy wave of homesickness. But she turned her attention to Kin Yang. What a surprise the man was. He was as thoughtful and polite as the other Chinese had been ruthless and disagreeable.

They found Yang's "humble" house to be a magnificent place, a glorious pattern of bamboo, teakwood, and silks. They were ushered into a room hung with beautiful tapestries, with incense curling from a brass image of Buddha, and a balcony from which, if they had taken the time, they could have seen much of the countryside. Women's outfits of red trousers and bright blue jackets were provided for the girls. They were thankful to get out of their dirty, stiff clothes.

Beverly giggled in delight as she viewed herself.

"Picture Larry in a skirt," she said to Shirley.

"Chinamen are funny," Shirley laughed. "The Chinaman wears a skirt while his wife wears the trousers."

A tinkling bell announced that it was time to dine and the girls, feeling self-conscious in their new wardrobe, went to join the others.

Kin Yang outdid himself in courtesy to the guests thrust so suddenly upon him. The meal was the best that could be prepared and, though it was undeniably oriental in flavor, the Americans thoroughly enjoyed it. Even music was supplied by three men with queer-looking Chinese instruments. Servants waited upon them deftly, noiselessly. Afterward Yang showed them some of his prized jade possessions.

They had not a moment to dwell upon thoughts of what a narrow escape they had had the night before. Too, they felt secure here in this household from any pursuit. Tomorrow they would be on their way to Canton.

"I didn't know a Chinaman could be so nice," Shirley sighed as the two girls went to their particular room just at sundown to rest. "The others we've met weren't so polite."

"Good and bad in all people," Beverly murmured, walking onto the balcony. "Look at the view, Shirley. The sunset is glorious."

The sky was a mass of colors.

"I wonder if Lois is painting it," Shirley murmured.

"We should be with them in a day or so," Beverly said. "Look at the bird!"

"Awk!" A screeching voice shrilled over the air.

Below them, a parrot perched on a low-hanging limb and squawked angrily at someone out of sight.

"Be still, John!" a voice commanded.

The parrot ruffled his feathers indignantly. His head twisted from side to side.

"I didn't see him before," Shirley said. "I wonder if he belongs to Kin Yang?"

As if in answer to her question a man limped out from the shadow of the house and the parrot hopped onto his shoulder.

"Evidently Yang has more company," Beverly said, straightening up as the parrot and his master disappeared from view. Suddenly she was all attention, staring to the south, toward the river. Her hand gripped Shirley's arm tensely. "Look, Shirley!" she commanded. "See it?"

"The 'Susabella'!" Shirley cried joyfully.

Over the tips of the trees could be seen the two flags at the masthead of the yacht. There could be no mistaking the Stars and Stripes that floated so vividly in the breeze or the other flag containing Roger's own private emblem for his boat.

"I wonder if it has been there all this time?" Shirley demanded.

"We didn't look out the window before," Beverly said, whirling and dashing from the room. "Let's go!"

With undignified haste the two girls dashed through the house, thoroughly destroying the oriental calm and peace with their eagerness. Rushing unceremoniously through the door Beverly collided with another figure.

It was the man with the parrot and at the accident the parrot squawked angrily and flew to a safe position atop a teakwood cabinet. Confusedly murmuring a few words of excuse, Beverly continued in her flight, Shirley at her heels.

Behind them the parrot bawled: "Pretty girl! Pretty girl!"

"Whoa! Wait a minute!"

Larry appeared suddenly in their path and caught each of them by an arm.

"What's the hurry? Where are you going? The pirates aren't after you!"

"The 'Susabella'," Beverly said, dancing impatiently. "We saw it from our balcony. It is anchored to the south of the village."

Larry took a hand of each.

"We're off!" he grinned and started forward, setting the pace.

They dashed madly through the little village, occupants of which regarded them wide-eyed. A few mongrel dogs barked and snapped at their heels but they did not slacken their pace.

"We forgot Woo Fong," Larry panted.

"You can go back for him," Shirley said generously.

They came upon the riverbank suddenly. Between them and the yacht, riding at anchor on the river, yawned what seemed a tremendous distance of water.

Shirley viewed it with dismay.

"I refuse to swim!" she stated positively after a glance at Beverly and Larry.

There was a raft tied to a stake driven into the ground. Larry looked at it, picked up the pole used for propelling the homemade craft, weighed it in his hand, and looked at the girls.

"It will do," Beverly said stepping onto the roughly hewn boat.

"If it will hold all of us," Shirley said.

"It wouldn't if Woo Fong was here," Larry laughed. "He's too heavy for a mere raft. All aboard!" He untied the rope and the raft drifted from the shore.

Larry bent all his weight on the pole. Luckily the water was comparatively calm and his inexperience did not hinder their progress.

On board the "Susabella" Lenora leaned on the rail and watched the raft put out from the shore. The native clothes were clearly visible to her but she did not distinguish anything familiar about the faces in the distance. It was probably natives trying to sell something she decided and turned her attention to other things.

It was three days since the girls had gone off the yacht in company with the pirates. Roger had told Woo Fong they would wait four days. Three of them were already gone. Three days of suspense and anxiety. Anxiety doubled by the receipt of a note from the pirates last night. Roger and Jim were conferring with Terry and Paul again about what they should do. Should they wait the four days they had given Woo Fong or depart immediately for Canton and see if they could get the necessary money?

Lenora sighed and turned from the rail. She was anxious to leave this spot. It had become monotonous. Every morning they woke to the same scene. Every day brought no good news, only its share of worry and wonderment. Lenora had to admit that even her good spirits were strangely quiet these days. Lois, too, seemed to have lost all her good humor. Jim and Roger hardly ever spoke at all. Terry and Paul and Miss Ernwood tried to be cheerful but were not very successful.

Slowly Lenora walked the length of the deck and turned to the companionway. The natives on the raft were coming closer now. She would go down and tell the others to come up and see them.

"I've seen too many natives already," Lois said.

"Tell them to go away," was Roger's comment.

Lenora sank onto the arm of Terry's chair.

"Tell them yourself. They will probably go when they don't see anybody on deck."

"A fine reception this is!" Shirley commented as they climbed aboard the "Susabella."

"We'll surprise them," Beverly plotted. "Not a sound now!"

On tiptoe the three descended the companionway. They appeared simultaneously in the lounge with cries of "Surprise!"

The young people gathered there stared for a moment and then with one accord they fell upon the three. Not for long months had the "Susabella" rung with such shouts of joy. It was almost worth all they had suffered to have the joy of return. Once more the "Susabella" could sail with all hands on board, gay and carefree. But they were soon to discover their troubles were not over. They were to meet Black Barney and Count Alexis again!

CHAPTER XIV

Shanghai

THAT VERY EVENING the young people made a journey to the home of Kin Yang to thank him for his hospitality and to find Woo Fong, without whom they could not possibly start their journey to Shanghai. The retired merchant was politeness itself and insisted upon all of them drinking a cup of tea to seal their friendship.

It was over the tea that Shirley asked:

"What happened to the parrot and that queer little man we bumped into?"

The merest flutter of an eyelash in Larry's direction betrayed Kin Yang, yet he answered suavely:

"I most humbly beg your pardon but there has been a mistake. Often birds fly into my garden of whom I know nothing."

"But the man was right here in the hall——" Shirley began in surprise.

The faintest pressure on her foot told her that Beverly wanted to attract her attention.

"Perhaps I was wrong," Shirley said and subsided, but she knew there had been a parrot and there had been a man. Beverly had almost knocked the man down when she ran into him!

As soon as they courteously could, the party took their leave and, with Woo Fong trailing along behind, made their way back to the "Susabella."

"Evelything topside?" Woo Fong grinned at Roger as he came on deck beside his young master.

"Topside!" Roger agreed. "You may have your holiday any time you like, Woo Fong."

"Velly happy," Woo smiled. "You like coffee and nice lemon pie?"

Lenora giggled.

"If we eat pie at this hour we will dream of pirates again."

"Just the same," Lois interrupted, "I'm hungry."

"Sandwiches and coffee in the lounge, Woo," Roger said. "I suppose you want to sail immediately, too?"

"Yes!" There was a chorus of affirmatives.

The anchor was duly hoisted and with a last look for the roof of Kin Yang's hospitable abode, which towered just above the trees on the hill, the young people said good-by to the place where so much had happened to them and turned their faces toward new and exciting scenes beckoning on ahead.

Beverly and Jim stood side by side in the bow. The air was gloriously cool but they welcomed it.

Quite suddenly Beverly turned around and found the deck deserted. They were alone. The others must have gone below. Yes, she could hear Larry's laugh intermingled with Lenora's.

Larry was sailing to Shanghai with them. Once there he would pursue his own business, the secret business which had brought him to the East. Beverly supposed he would continue on the trail of Black Barney, and whether they would see him again she did not know. Larry had been a great comfort in the days just past. He was gay, carefree, reckless, even rash sometimes, but he had the knack of getting out of tight places unscathed. He was always good company, and he had certainly been a pillar of strength when they were in the pirate camp. Without him they would not be here now, safe and sound. He had jeopardized his own job—even his life—helping them.

"Of what are you thinking?" Jim asked, smiling down at her.

"What? Oh—the pirates," she said at length. "I wonder if Black Barney has given up?"

"Never fear," Jim laughed. "We will see him again."

"Does your shoulder hurt much?" She laid her hand lightly on his arm.

"Nary a bit—now," he said. "Beverly——"

She turned about quickly. "Where is everybody? Where's Shirley?"

"Down in the lounge I suppose," Jim replied.

"Woo Fong ought to have his sandwiches made by this time," Beverly said. "Let's go down."

He followed her across the deck and down the companionway. The others were all in the lounge. Woo Fong was just setting down his tray containing two large plates of sandwiches and a silver coffee urn. Without more ado Lenora became very attentive to the plate of sandwiches.

"I've been thinking," she said at length, her mouth full.

"Don't," Lois counseled. "It might bring on another hurricane."

Lenora ignored her. She perched on the arm of Terry's chair and gave him her coffee cup to hold.

"Oh, I say!" Terry protested.

"I have a declaration of war to make," Lenora continued sublimely.

"War?" Shirley asked lazily.

She was sitting in a long deck chair and she felt too comfortable to move. Roger supplied her with sandwiches and coffee.

"War!" Lenora repeated firmly. "Also, it may lead to riches—undying fame—adventure in the heart of the wilds——"

"What *are* you talking about?" Lois demanded in exasperation.

"A treasure hunt," Lenora said in a dramatic whisper.

"With what as the treasure?" Beverly wanted to know.

"Whatever Jim's map leads us to," Lenora explained. "Now wait a minute," she continued hastily as Roger started to speak. "I know we only have half of it. So far Black Barney has been trying to get that. Now my suggestion is that we bestir ourselves and give him some action. Why don't we try to get the map from him? We have more right to the map than he has. Slim told Jim the treasure was his—if he could find it. It would be no end thrilling. It might lead us to a diamond mine—or something."

"Or something," Terry said dryly.

"It would also lead us into a lot of trouble," Lois added.

"Trouble!" Lenora dismissed that with a snap of her fingers. "After we have been kidnaped by pirates and all what is trouble to us?"

"We are the ones who were kidnaped, and personally I'm not looking for any more trouble," Shirley sighed. "What do you think, Beverly?"

Beverly grinned. "Strange as it may seem, I am inclined to agree with Lenora."

"Hurrah!" Lenora shouted. "One ally in my cause."

"I think it is time we did something besides run away from Barney and the Count," Beverly continued. "Besides, as Lenora says, it might lead to a lot of adventures."

"All you have to do is find Barney and Count what's-his-name," Larry said.

"That's where you come in," Beverly said brightly.

"If you are still concerned with Barney, then you can always tell us where he is."

"No thanks," Larry declined. "I'm saying good-by to you in Shanghai—much as I hate to do it," he added gallantly.

"I think we should leave well enough alone," Roger contributed.

"Beverly," Lenora wailed, "can't you say something to persuade them?"

"We can always go ourselves," Beverly murmured.

"Go where?" Jim asked suspiciously.

"Wherever Barney goes," Lenora supplied. "We shall be prepared to fare forth in search of fame and fortune at scarcely a moment's notice. 'Beware of Barney' shall be our watchword."

"Someone should warn the poor man," Lois declared; "with two such relentless bloodhounds on his trail——"

"And remember," Lenora continued, "we won't even give you a smell of the treasure when we find it."

"Well, in that case," Lois grinned, "maybe I'll join forces with you."

"I think you are all a little mad," Roger declared, pulling Shirley to her feet. He led the way up onto the deck and the others straggled after.

It was late but none of them felt like sleeping.

"Do you think we should set a guard against any future pirates?" Jim asked.

"I've already done that," Roger said, indicating

the two members of the crew who were stationed one on each side of the boat.

"We don't want any more sneaking up on us," Lenora grimaced.

Lenora and Terry were leaning against the rail a little apart from the others. A hoarse voice spoke behind them.

"Pretty girl! Pretty girl!"

"Oh, thank you!" Lenora giggled. "Terry, you say the nicest things."

Terry laughed. "I didn't say that."

"None of us did," Lois added as she and Paul strolled up.

"Pretty girl!" The exclamation was repeated.

They began looking about, puzzled as to where the voice came from.

"Shirley——" Beverly began.

"At Kin Yang's!" Shirley put in eagerly. "When we were running from the house——"

"What is this all about?" Paul demanded.

Shirley and Beverly were moving about, gazing into most unusual places.

"Do you think it will snow?" Lenora wanted to know, as Shirley strained her eyes upward, looking toward the stars where the flags fluttered from a mast.

"Look! Bev, there it is!" Shirley exclaimed. "Get him, somebody."

In the darkness the mere shadow of the bird at the mast was visible. It was the same parrot they had seen at Kin Yang's. They had recognized his voice when he shouted "Pretty girl!" just as they had heard him do before.

"Pretty bird!" Lois called.

"Come on down," added Lenora. She whistled ineffectively. The other's coaxing was equally fruitless. The parrot strutted up and down the mast but he remained safely out of reach.

Roger started determinedly to climb the pole. The others cheered him on with various shouts, but, just as he came within reach of the bird, the parrot squawked and fluttered to the flag pole at the stern. The sailor stationed there reached for the bird but missed and fell into the water.

Hastily the others went to rescue the young man. The parrot squawked encouragement to the man in the water.

"That bird is a heartless wretch!" Lenora declared, leaning over the rail.

"Awk!" replied the bird. "Pretty girl!"

"Well," Lenora smiled, "after such a compliment I'll forgive him."

"He didn't mean you," Lois retorted. "How will we catch him?"

"Doesn't anyone have a net or something?" Larry asked.

"The net from the ping-pong table!" Paul said and departed. He returned a few moments later with the net tied onto a yardstick. But it was too small to be effective.

"Get a pillowcase," Shirley advised.

Jim and Roger armed themselves with self-made nets of pillowcases, but it took them quite a while to catch the bird. The parrot fluttered from perch to perch, eluding them and screaming at the top of his lungs.

With a leap and sweep of the pillowcase Jim lunged after the bird as he was making for the mast again. Just as the pillowcase slipped over the bird's head Jim tripped and brought both of them crashing to the deck.

"You'll squash the poor bird!" Lenora cried.

"He deserves to be squashed after all the trouble he caused," Lois declared.

The bird was making a great hullabaloo and doing his best to escape from the confines of the pillowcase. They brought him out and kept a secure hold upon him while they tied a piece of strong string on one of his legs. However, it seemed he realized that he was caught at last and, perching docilely upon Lenora's shoulder, he made no attempt to escape.

"Where did he come from?" Lois wanted to know.

"We saw him in Kin Yang's," Shirley said. "That was the parrot I asked about."

"What happened to his owner?" Lenora pursued.

"You heard Kin Yang say he didn't know a thing about either of them," Shirley said abruptly.

"I wonder what his name is," Paul murmured,

poking a finger experimentally in the bird's direction.

"We heard someone call him John," Shirley continued.

"John!" Larry blurted out.

The others looked at him queerly, he had seemed so surprised. Beverly was sure he had recognized the name, for now he eyed the parrot with new interest.

"Yes, John. Why?"

"Oh—it seems a strange name for a bird," Larry murmured. "What do you intend to do with him?"

"Take him back with us to America," Lenora declared. "Aren't we, John?"

"Pretty girl!" John replied promptly.

"That is why she wants him," Lois laughed. "He flatters her."

"Parrots are notoriously truthful," Lenora declared haughtily.

"That narrow band on his other leg puzzles me," Roger said. "I wonder if he carries messages?"

Larry bent over the bird, his fingers twirling the gold band on the bird's left leg. Pulling and twisting, Larry took the band off and not one of those present noticed the small slip of paper that was transferred surreptitiously into his coat pocket. A few moments later he excused himself from the party and made his way to the cabin he shared with Jim and Roger. There he unfolded the tiny paper and read it several times. Finally he touched a match to it and watched the message burn to crisp blackness.

Shanghai was but another surprise on top of all they had had so far. Heretofore, when they had spoken of China, while at home in America, it had been with various flights of fancy. Certainly they had not expected such an Americanized scene.

They gazed in surprise at the tall, foreign buildings, mostly offices and hotels; at the well-policed streets; and, in the business sections, at red and green traffic lights!

There were churches, parks, and race courses. At the race course, in the International Settlement, everything from races to football was played. At night they found theater and social functions galore.

The suburbs had many beautiful villas with spacious lawns and shade trees.

But the part that especially appealed to them was the native city. They left the wide, well-paved streets of the International Settlement and followed the crowded, narrow thoroughfares. Few foreigners were to be seen. There were shops on every hand. On one street they seemed to sell nothing but birds. The little feathered songsters in their bamboo cages were displayed in nearly every shop. Lenora considered getting a playmate for John but the others restrained her.

Lenora and Terry insisted upon visiting the famous teahouse built over the water. Farther on were the temple and pagoda Paul and Lois wanted to see. Roger, Shirley, Beverly, and Jim decided to wander about aimlessly through the city.

They went into one shop and gazed around. A string of blue glass beads attracted Shirley's attention, not that she really wanted them so much, merely as an additional souvenir. But she decided the price put upon them by the native merchant was too high.

They turned to go out when a voice, harsh and deep, called from beyond the tapestry that divided the shop into two rooms.

"Yin! Yin Loo! Where are you?"

The merchant bowed to his late customers and hurried off.

Shirley and Beverly exchanged frightened glances. The same thought was in the mind of each. Black Barney was in Shanghai—in this very building!

"B-Beverly, do—do you hear that?" Shirley managed to whisper.

"What about it?" Jim asked.

"That's Barney," Beverly told him in a low voice. "I'd know that voice anywhere."

"Let's get out of here," Shirley added, pulling Roger after her toward the door.

"So Barney is in Shanghai!" Jim said grimly. "I knew we would meet him again."

"I hope he doesn't know we are here," Shirley shivered. "Let's sail tonight!"

"No!" Beverly said firmly. "On the boat we said we wouldn't run away from him anymore. Every time we are enjoying a place he pops up and we have to leave. We will stay in Shanghai!"

"B-but B-Barney——" Shirley began.

Jim put a comforting hand beneath her arm. "We'll keep him away from you."

Beverly turned to Roger. "Let's go back and wait until he comes out and then follow him."

"Oh, no," Roger protested. "That would be inviting trouble."

"Well, why not?" Beverly demanded irritably. "Aren't we going to do anything?"

"You girls are going safely back to the yacht," Roger said firmly, and Jim nodded in agreement.

"I don't want to be safe and sound every minute!" Beverly protested.

"Just the same, you are going to be," Roger and Jim said together firmly.

Beverly said no more but there was a dangerous glint in her eyes. As she looked away from her friends to the crowded shops her mind was busily devising ways and means. If the others had noticed the set line of her chin and the determined light in her eyes they would have been more worried. When Beverly was so indomitable things were bound to happen.

They found Lenora and Terry had already returned to the yacht and the former was ready to burst into tears.

"What's wrong?" Shirley wanted to know.

"John is gone," Lenora wailed. "We came back and he was gone."

"Did he fly away?" Beverly asked.

"I had him in my cabin," Lenora continued. "He isn't there now and he isn't anywhere on the boat."

They searched systematically for the parrot but it was as Lenora had said. He was nowhere on the boat. He had disappeared completely and secretly.

Lois and Paul returned shortly and Miss Ernwood sent word that she was dining with friends at the American Consul's. That left the young people to their own devices for the evening.

"I want to go to the movies!" Lenora declared vigorously.

They dressed for the evening, dined at a famous restaurant and went on to a theater showing American films which Lenora had discovered.

Sitting in the dark beside Lenora, Beverly whispered to her friend the fact that Barney was in Shanghai. They had neglected to tell their friends of the discovery of the afternoon.

"What?" Lenora spoke aloud and several people turned to stare at her. "Where?" she continued in a whisper.

Beverly told her all that had happened.

"Why didn't you stay and follow him?" Lenora asked excitedly. "I would have."

"I'll meet him again," Beverly said grimly. "Either him or the Count."

After the theater they took their way leisurely back to the yacht. The boat was in darkness, everyone busy on shore.

Lenora was first down the companionway. She stepped into the lounge and gave a shout. Furniture had been overturned, pictures ripped from their frames, every conceivable place where a bit of paper may have been hidden was torn asunder.

They found each cabin in the same condition. Trunks and suitcases had been slashed, drawers and closets turned out, even the bunks had been torn apart.

"Look at this!" Roger shouted.

Tacked on the inside of his door was a slip of paper and printed thereon in crude lettering were three words: "Remember the Si!"

"The pirates on the Si River!" Lois said in an awe-stricken voice.

"Barney!" Lenora and Beverly exclaimed together.

"Well?" Lenora continued imperiously. "Are you going to stand for this? I told you we should have declared war on them."

"This is too much," Shirley agreed. "Look at our things—we'll never be able to use our trunks or suitcases again!"

The four young men said nothing, merely helped the girls straighten the mess the pirates had caused—if it were pirates.

"I wonder if Larry has found Barney," Beverly murmured as she and Shirley tried to restore order to their cabin.

"Larry is queer," Shirley said. "He pops up in the most unexpected places——"

"Lucky for us," Beverly laughed. "I wonder if he has gone back to the States or stayed in China."

"Didn't he tell you where he was going?" Shirley asked.

"No."

Beverly was remembering Larry's expression when he first heard the name of the parrot which had appeared so strangely on their boat. It had been as if he recognized it. Too, he had been curiously reticent about his destination when he took farewell of them all on their arrival in Shanghai. He had merely said "Au revoir" and walked off the boat, disappearing into the milling crowd on the dock.

Yet, had she but known it, Larry was still in Shanghai. Still near to her and the others, and she was destined to meet him again very soon.

The next morning Lenora came to the breakfast table with the expressed desire to ride in a wheelbarrow.

"Take a cushion along," Lois advised.

In the town vehicles to be chosen by tourists consisted of almost any sort of conveyance, including rickshas and wheelbarrows. Lenora had the idea that her visit would not be complete without a ride in the latter.

"Terry," Lenora coaxed, "go along? Let's go into town on a wheelbarrow. I want to get Connie a pair of ivory book ends I saw in the native section."

"All right," Terry sighed. "What are the others going to do?"

"Lois is going out to paint a picture of the tea-house built over the water," Paul contributed, "and I'm going along."

"I want to go to the race track," Beverly said. She cast a fleeting glimpse to where Shirley and Jim were bending over a map of the city, then she turned to Roger. "Be my escort?" she inquired brightly.

"Rather!" he agreed promptly. "I want to see those races, too."

Both Shirley and Jim looked up in surprise as Beverly and Roger promptly left the lounge. Paul, Lois, Lenora, and Terry followed.

"Well——" Shirley began.

Jim grinned ruefully. "Sort of leaves us to our own resources. What shall we do?"

"Why not go with me to the British Embassy?" Miss Ernwood inquired. "There is a tea party there this afternoon."

A tea party did not exactly appeal to the young people's adventurous desires but nevertheless they agreed.

Beverly and Roger started out gaily. They had always been good companions and now Beverly felt that Shirley would be able to spend the whole day with Jim. She had not forgotten what had happened on the pirate junk. Every time Shirley referred to Jim, Beverly was sure it was with more than friendliness. She was willing to do anything to increase their happiness because they were both her best friends.

The races that afternoon were exciting, every one

a test of excellent horsemanship. The horses were thoroughbreds and, with each striving in true thoroughbred fashion, it made the races close, the winner emerging victorious only by the barest margin.

Roger, his hat pushed onto the back of his head, cheered lustily. It was impossible for Beverly not to catch some of his enthusiasm.

"I'll bet you on this one," Roger proposed. "A cigarette case against——"

"A pair of earrings!" Beverly agreed eagerly. "I choose the blue and white colors."

"The red and white will win!" Roger declared confidently.

Beverly's choice was a brown-and-white bit of streaked lightning, but it soon became apparent that Roger's coal-black two-year-old did not intend to be among the tardy ones in coming in to the finish line. The crowd was jumping, shouting, cheering itself hoarse.

"I'm going to like that cigarette case," Roger laughed.

"Not half as much as I will my earrings," Beverly shot back promptly.

Neck and neck three horses bid for the lead as they rounded the last turn.

"Come on, red and white!" Roger was yelling, waving his hat.

The black horse was edging ahead of the other two. Bit by bit the jockey in blue and white coaxed his horse up. The black and the brown and white horses raced toward the finish line, manes flying, jockeys clinging, urging, dust flying.

"It's going to be a tie!" Roger predicted with a sigh.

"The blue and white—he's gaining!" Beverly cried in delight.

The strong pace was telling on the black horse. He kept his fast stride, but the brown-and-white horse increased his a mite. Inch by inch he pulled a whole head in front of the black horse.

The race was over in a cloud of dust and a chorus of cheers from the spectators. The brown-and-white horse, carrying his jockey proudly displaying his blue and white colors, had won.

"Now we'll go and buy my earrings," Beverly said practically.

"I still say the black is the best horse," Roger declared, grinning.

A moment more and all thought of earrings had completely gone from Beverly's head. In the crowd, as they were leaving the race track, Beverly caught sight of a familiar face. She stopped in her pace and grasped Roger's arm.

"Look!" she whispered. "Count Alexis!"

"Where?" Roger looked around eagerly. "I'm anxious to meet that fellow."

"There," Beverly said. "He's getting into that ricksha!"

"We'll do likewise," Roger proposed.

Beverly and Roger settled in rickshas and Roger

gave instructions to follow the Count "Chop chop!"

"Chop chop!" the coolies agreed with a grin and the ricksha rolled away.

They came to the native quarter and it was impossible to go any farther in their vehicles. The coolies were paid and dismissed. When the Count left his ricksha and strolled along the narrow street they were but a few paces behind him. Once he stopped to look into a shop. They did not want to pass him, so they stopped, too. Roger made a pretext of giving a few pennies to a beggar. Then they went on.

The Count was evidently in no hurry. He stopped often to peer into shops, examining and bargaining.

Once, marking time while they waited for the Count to emerge from a jade shop, Beverly bought a large lotus flower from a thin and ragged street urchin.

The youngster pushed the flower into her hand and disappeared. Beverly looked down in surprise. With the flower in her hand lay a small bit of folded paper.

"Look," she whispered to Roger. "What do you suppose it is?"

"It's a note evidently," Roger said. "Read it."

Beverly unfolded the paper and read the few words written in a familiar hand. The message was very brief and to the point:

"Stay out of the native city!"

"That's strange," Roger murmured. "I wonder who's warning us?"

"It's Larry's handwriting," Beverly said. "He's written to me often. I'd recognize it anywhere. But," she looked about at the unfamiliar faces, "I wonder how he knew how to find us?"

"Here comes the Count," Roger said. "Come along."

"Do you think we should?" Beverly hesitated. "If Larry says to stay out of the native city there must be a reason."

"As long as we've come this far we might as well find out where he is going," Roger said determinedly.

"All right," Beverly sighed.

Larry's note served to lend an added zest to the chase. Beverly's better judgment told her to obey Larry's warning and depart forthwith. But the urge for adventure and danger was stronger. With a delicious thrill she stayed close to Roger and the two went on after Count Alexis.

CHAPTER XV

Warnings

THE SUNLIGHT touched the curved corners of the little teahouse roof with gold. Natives looked smilingly at Lois and Paul. The former was busy with her canvas and brush while Paul watched. A duplicate of the teahouse appeared on the sheet before her. Far into the afternoon Lois labored. Then Paul insisted they go in to the house and have a cup of tea.

They were served in little china cups decorated with cherry blossoms. The air was faintly scented with incense. They talked about their trip and lingered over the tea. The waiter brought their second pot of fresh tea and departed with a deferential bow. Lois lifted the teapot to pour and stopped in surprise. Beneath the teapot was a small bit of paper. She watched while Paul unfolded it wonderingly. Silently he passed it to her.

"Stay out of the native quarter!" she read.

"What does it mean?" she asked Paul.

"A warning," he said, sipping his tea. "But whether from friend or foe——"

Lois shivered suddenly. "Let's go back to the yacht."

The teahouse that had seemed so friendly a moment before had turned cold and hostile. Suddenly all the charm of Shanghai had vanished beneath a cloud of ominous possibilities.

Hastily Lois gathered her canvas and painting equipment together. They left the teahouse with scarcely a backward glance. Lois could not leave the native city fast enough. She was sure something dreadful would happen before they reached the "Susabella", but nothing did.

Lenora and Terry had a gay time poking around in the native shops. The day before, Lenora had seen a pair of ivory book ends which she had now decided she wanted for Connie. But, as usual with Lenora, she had forgotten in what shop she saw them. Therefore, there was nothing for them to do but go to all the shops again.

Lenora found Terry always good company. She delighted in teasing him for he never got angry. Since she had met him in England and they had spent so much time in each other's company she had come to like Terry a lot, but not for anything in the world would she have admitted it.

"Do you have to have that particular set of book

ends?" Terry asked wearily, when they had spent all morning in a fruitless search.

"Positively," Lenora said.

"What if they are already sold?"

"Hm, I hadn't thought of that," Lenora said. "Anyway, we'll look some more."

Along in the afternoon they came to a dark little shop and Lenora exclaimed in delight when she saw the particular book ends on display.

"At last!" she cried. "Terry, there they are."

"Don't let the man see that you want them very much," Terry advised, "or the price will go up."

Terry, experienced in the ways of the oriental shopkeepers, bargained wisely with the little Chinaman. The book ends passed into Lenora's possession.

When the man returned from the interior of his shop and handed the wrapped package to Terry the two immediately left. It was on the street that Terry noticed a folded piece of paper on top of the bundle.

"What's that?" Lenora asked.

Terry unfolded it and read aloud the few words printed thereon:

" 'Stay out of the native quarter!' "

The two exchanged glances.

"I say!" Terry gasped.

"L-let's go back to the yacht," Lenora proposed, casting an apprehensive glance over her shoulder.

"Where did it come from?" Terry wanted to know. "I'm certain it wasn't there when the shopkeeper gave me the package."

"N-never mind," Lenora said, tugging at his sleeve. "L-let's go back."

"We jolly well shall not!" Terry said staunchly, eyes twinkling mischievously. "We shall go right on——"

"Oh, no!" Lenora said firmly. "Sir Terence Cartwright! You take me back to the yacht now!"

Terry sighed. "I thought you wanted excitement. Here is your chance——"

"I've changed my mind," Lenora declared.

The strange yellow faces on each side of them had suddenly become hostile. Lenora could fancy threatening glances cast in their direction.

Coming out onto the dock Lenora clutched at Terry's arm.

"There's John—the parrot!" Lenora cried excitedly.

A small wiry man turned away from his contemplation of the water. On his shoulder perched a parrot.

The three came face to face for only an instant. Then the little man was stepping aside to let the young man and woman pass. But Lenora did not intend to pass. She reached out a hand toward the bird.

"John! You naughty bird! Where have you been?"

"Shiver my timbers!" the parrot squawked in the vernacular of the sea.

"Sorry, Miss," the little man touched his seaman's cap politely. "You've made a mistake——"

"See here," Terry interrupted, "isn't this bird's name John?"

"No, sir!" the man replied promptly.

"It is!" Lenora insisted. "John"—she ruffled the parrot's feathers with a finger and hastily withdrew her hand as the bird pecked at it—"John, who is it, John? Who is it, John?"

The parrot twisted his head to one side, his eyes glaring at her.

"Who is it, John?" Lenora insisted.

"Pretty girl!" the bird replied loudly.

"I knew it!" Lenora turned jubilantly to Terry. "John always said that when you asked him who was talking."

But the second that Lenora turned to Terry the little man turned and hurried away. He was rapidly disappearing into the crowd when Lenora and Terry hurried after. Agile though they were, the little man eluded them and was lost completely. Disgruntled and disappointed Lenora and Terry returned to the dock and went on board the yacht.

"We'll have to go around questioning all the parrots in sight," Terry sighed.

"You will be arrested going around speaking to strange birds," Lois giggled when the incident was recounted to her.

Shirley and Jim dutifully accompanied Miss Ernwood to tea at the Embassy. They met countless personages, were very, very polite, and drank cups and cups of tea. Along about the middle of the party Jim began to get restless. Shirley could sympathize with him but that was all. They had to grin and bear it.

"If I have to be polite to one more person or drink one more cup of tea I shall smash something!" Jim threatened in Shirley's ear.

"I've an idea," Shirley murmured.

"What is it?" he asked eagerly.

"Hasn't it seemed strange to you that there are no young people in the room?" Shirley demanded in a whisper. "There were three young men and two girls here when we came. Several have come in since. They stay for a moment and then disappear. Where do they go?"

"Home probably," Jim said gloomily. "Let's go back to the yacht without Miss Ernwood."

"We can't," Shirley protested. "Instead, let's go hunting!"

"Tigers or elephants?"

"You go out that door there." Shirley motioned toward the door at the farther end of the room. "I'll slip out the other one in a few moments and meet you in the hall."

"I'm on my way," Jim said immediately.

Shirley watched his tall figure mingle with the army uniforms, tailored suits and afternoon gowns, and then disappear through the farther door. Leisurely she sauntered toward the door. Once she was detained by a visiting missionary who was sure she had met Shirley in New York.

At last with a deep sigh of relief Shirley came out into the large reception hall which was almost deserted now. Jim was pacing the tile floor, his brow as black as a thundercloud.

"I thought you'd never come!" he said.

"I thought I'd never get here, too," she agreed. "Did you ever meet so many staid and respectable people in your life?"

"Never!" Jim declared solemnly. "What shall we do now? Couldn't we possibly get our hats and coats and——"

"By Jove! What a small world this is!" A hearty voice boomed behind the two Americans.

Exchanging exasperated glances Jim and Shirley turned to see what new bore was descending upon them. But the moment they caught sight of the stocky figure their faces cleared and they actually smiled.

"Mr. Anton!" Shirley exclaimed.

"None other!" the explorer grinned, shaking hands with Jim.

It was the same man whom they had met in India when he returned with Beverly to Sir Reginald's bungalow after the boat accident.

"What are you doing in Shanghai?" Shirley asked gaily.

"Just got in this morning," he said. "Finished my business in India and am on my way home to the States. Thought I'd take a little vacation here first, though."

"Tell us about your explorations," Jim proposed,
drawing him toward a window seat.

"Not now, old chap," Anthony Anton murmured.
"Aren't you guests at the tea party?"

Shirley and Jim nodded in unison.

"Worse luck!" added Jim. "We were about to run
away."

"Bored?"

"Bored to tears," Shirley confided.

"Hm." Anthony Anton cast a humorous glance
toward the room from which came the tinkle of
china cups and the buzz of low, polite conversation.

"Why don't you go up to Lottie's room?"

"Is it any worse than that?" Jim demanded suspiciously.

"Where is it?" Shirley asked.

Anthony Anton laughed. "That is where all the
young people usually congregate. It is upstairs toward
the back of the house—well out of earshot," he added
with a wink. "Wait for me while I speak to a few
people and I'll take you up. You'll like it," he declared.

Jim and Shirley sat together on the window seat.
They had a view overlooking a garden and an artificial lake where lotus flowers were wont to bloom.

"I hope he isn't long," Shirley sighed.

Jim glanced at his watch. "We've only been here
two hours but it seems like six."

It really did not take the explorer long to pay his
respects to his acquaintances but it seemed long to

the young people waiting. He came and led the way up the circular staircase to the second floor. They walked along the carpeted corridor and as they drew near the back of the house unmistakable sounds of hilarity met them.

Anthony Anton grinned. "Lottie is having a grand party, I'll wager. You'll meet the liveliest group in Shanghai here. The Ambassador's daughter knows everybody and his brother."

"Won't she mind our walking in like this?" Shirley asked a bit timidly.

"Not at all," the man declared. "She'll welcome you with open arms. Living in Shanghai, Lottie is anxious to meet all the newcomers. She will bombard you with questions at first, but you will like her," he predicted.

Coming to a closed door at the farthest end of the hall he beat a light tattoo upon it with his fingers. It was flung open immediately. They could see a great many people crowded into a small room. A piano was doing its duty while a group of girls were singing. At the same time a radio sent forth a low, pleasant hum of melody.

The two Americans were indeed welcomed in a most friendly manner. There was no restraint here among the younger set. Anthony Anton was welcomed hilariously. Evidently he was an honored member of the set. As his friends, the young man and woman were drawn immediately into the circle of gay life.

"Not a bad party after all," Jim beamed at Shirley, a half hour later, during a momentary lull.

"We'll teach Beverly and Roger to go to the races without us," added Shirley.

"I'm certainly glad Mr. Anton came in when he did!" declared Jim.

Songs were sung, stories told, experiences exchanged, and then the writer-explorer held them enthralled with the tale of his discovery of a ruined temple in India.

After Mr. Anton's story was told a young naval officer suggested that they go in a body to a little restaurant in the native city for their dinner.

The suggestion was hailed with enthusiasm. Immediately they scattered to claim their wraps and agreed to meet outside.

Jim and Shirley sought out Miss Ernwood, acquainted her with their plans, and departed to get their wraps.

Jim assisted Shirley into her coat and turned to put on his hat. They hurried outside and met Mr. Anton.

"Queer decorations you wear in your hat," the explorer laughed.

"What?" Jim took off his hat. In the band was sticking a white piece of paper. He pulled it out and read it. He crumpled the note in his hand and grinned ruefully at Mr. Anton.

"We won't be able to join the party. I'm terribly sorry, really. Thank Lottie for a grand time for us, will you? If you can, come down to the yacht before you sail for home. The others would like to see you I'm sure. Good-by, old chap!"

Jim hurried Shirley away and left the explorer staring after them in surprise. His words had been so unexpected Mr. Anton had not had a chance to protest.

"What's the matter with you?" Shirley demanded when they were out of earshot and Jim was propelling her rapidly along the street. "We had a chance to join such a grand party and you——"

"Read this," Jim commanded, putting into her hand the note that had been stuck in his hat band.

Shirley unfolded the paper and read the words:

"Stay out of the native city!"

"Someone is trying to scare us," she laughed.

"Perhaps!" Jim said a bit grimly. "But we aren't taking any chances. At least you aren't," he amended. "We're going back to the yacht."

"But I don't want to go back there," Shirley protested. "I want to go on the party with Lottie and Mr. Anton."

"No can do," Jim said sternly. "We are going back to the 'Susabella' and see if any of the others got one of these notes."

"Who put it in your hat?" Shirley wanted to know.

"If we knew that we would know if it was from friend or foe," Jim said. "Somebody might be giving us good advice, and on the other hand——"

"It might be just a joke," Shirley said.

They hurried from the scene of the party back to

the dock. It was growing dark swiftly now and lights twinkled at them from the craft anchored there.

Lois, Paul, Lenora, and Terry were at the rail to greet them when they came on board.

"Greetings!" Lenora waved a half-demolished cookie in their direction. "What kind of a time did you have today and did you receive any mysterious notes?"

"We did!" Jim replied promptly.

"Did you?" added Shirley.

"We each did," Paul said. "Who do you suppose they are from?"

"The writing on ours seems familiar"—Shirley puckered her brow thoughtfully—"but I can't place it. I thought one of you might be playing a trick on us."

"Not guilty!" Lenora declared.

"We wouldn't send one to ourselves at the same time," Lois said indignantly when Shirley eyed her suspiciously.

"Then who did?" Shirley wanted to know.

"Wait until I tell you!" Lenora exclaimed. She pulled Shirley down beside her on the wicker divan. "We saw John!"

"John who?" Shirley asked innocently.

"John, 'Pretty girl'," Lois mimicked. "The parrot. Only it wasn't John," she added with a grin for Lenora. "The man who had the bird must have thought you were crazy."

Lenora made a little face at her.

"I'm convinced someone stole John," she declared firmly. "And I think it was that little man. I didn't like his looks."

"He must have sailed the sea for a great many years," Terry said. "He looked like an old salt."

Sitting on deck, waiting for Roger and Beverly to return, they exchanged the day's experiences. Chinese lanterns were lighted, fore and aft. They swung gently to and fro in the night air. Lenora turned on the radio and she and Terry danced.

"I wish they would come," Lois grumbled. "I want my dinner."

"At last!" Lenora shouted. "Someone, beside me, is hungry."

"You shouldn't be hungry," Terry grinned down at her. "You've been eating ever since we came back to the boat."

"I have not!" Lenora denied. "I haven't eaten a thing for at least twenty minutes."

"A world's record!" Paul laughed.

"Listen!" Shirley commanded. "Isn't that a motorboat coming out from the shore?"

"A motorboat, no less?" Lenora cried. "This morning they left the 'Susabella' in a rowboat."

"Miracles do happen in the Orient," Paul confided.

The motorboat pulled along side of the yacht. They could see several people standing, waving to them. It did not take long for the new arrivals to climb aboard the yacht.

The first one to step forward was Anthony Anton.

After him came Lottie, the Ambassador's daughter, and following her were the three young naval officers Jim and Shirley had met that afternoon.

"Since you wouldn't join our party," Lottie laughed, "we brought the party to you."

"You'll have to explain yourself," Mr. Anton declared to Jim when he had greeted the others and his companions had been introduced. "Why did you run away?"

"Well, you see, that bit of paper someone stuck in my hat was a mysterious note. It warned us to stay away from the native city. We came back to the yacht to see if any of the others had received a similar one," Jim explained.

"It sounds thrilling," Lottie declared. "But why should you receive a mysterious note?"

"Do you have any enemies in China?" a naval man asked.

"We have an enemy who follows us around the world," Lenora told him with her most bewitching smile, for the young man was very handsome in his uniform. "Wherever we go—he goes, too."

"I say!" Another officer came to Lenora's side. "Who is the fellow?"

Lois prodded Shirley in the ribs and grinned:

"Lenora is surrounded by the navy."

"Well, now that you know nothing has happened here at the boat, you will go on to dinner with us, won't you?" Lottie dimpled at Jim. "We promised to meet the rest of the group."

"Shall we?" Jim asked his American friends.

"I'd love it!" Lenora declared, smiling at the naval officers.

Terry, witnessing Lenora's complete absorption in the pride of the navy, philosophically attached himself to Lottie.

"What about Beverly and Roger?" Shirley asked.

"We don't know where they are," Lenora shrugged. "I, for one, am not in favor of waiting for them. They may not be back for hours. They probably went to the theater—or something."

"I agree with Lenora," Lois said. "Let's go to dinner by all means."

"We'll make a night of it!" Lottie cried gaily.

With that they could agree. They were in the mood for fast and furious fun. Under the guidance of Lottie, one well-versed in Shanghai's points of interest, they could not fail to have the time of their lives. It promised much more entertainment than remaining on the yacht.

"Where are we going?" Shirley asked as she climbed aboard the motorboat beside Lottie.

"To Charlie Wong's," Lottie said promptly. "My friends said they would wait there for us. Of course, we might only start there," she added. "We shall dedicate ourselves to showing you a side of China you probably have not seen yet."

"It will be fascinating," Lenora prophesied. With a tall, impressive, and handsome ensign on each side of her she was sure the evening would be a success.

Perhaps it was the white, smart caps, the gold buttons—at any rate, uniforms always "did" something to Lenora. She smiled mischievously at Terry. She knew that young man was probably furious with her for paying so much attention to the navy men. Nevertheless, she was enjoying herself. Not even Terry's disapproval could cause her a moment's regret.

The boat covered the distance from the yacht to the dock rapidly. Only that morning the Captain had moved the yacht out a short distance from the dock. They felt the separation of water gave them a bit more privacy. They could never accustom themselves to the prying eyes peering at them from the queer little junks as they drifted past. Off from the shore it gave them a better view of the shore line and ships, coming from all ports of the world, to anchor here in this port of the East.

The happy group made a good deal of noise when they landed on the dock. Hilariously they went off together and not one of them noticed the tanned, wiry little man standing in the shadows, a bird perched upon his shoulder. Thoughtfully he watched them disappear, then turned to stare out over the water to where the "Susabella" rode gently on the swell of the waves. Then, pulling his peaked cap a little lower over his eyes and shifting the bird to his other shoulder, he hurried off after the group of young people.

CHAPTER XVI

Charlie Wong's

WITH apprehension growing in her heart, Beverly followed Roger as they kept within sight of Count Alexis. Larry's note perplexed her. Why should he send them such a warning? Was it possible anyone had copied his handwriting to mislead them? That was too imaginative, she told herself. There would be no reason for anyone to do such a thing. She would accept the fact that Larry had sent them a warning. Why should he send it? What was there to warn them about?

Had Larry discovered that the Count and Barney were in Shanghai? Were they at this very moment plotting some danger against the young people on board the "Susabella"? After the fruitless search last night, Barney would be raving. She could picture his anger when, after all their trouble, they had discovered nothing.

The street was filled with jostling crowds. Beverly

and Roger had a hard time to keep from being separated. Once they had to flatten themselves against a building to let a Chinaman, balancing his shoulder poles, pass.

The Count disappeared into a store and they could see him in the dim interior arguing with the proprietor when they slowly sauntered past.

"Now is your chance to go back to the 'Susabella'," Roger said.

"And leave you?" Beverly asked suspiciously.

"I'm going to follow the Count," Roger said determinedly. "But I want you to go back to the boat."

"Why?" Beverly demanded.

"It isn't safe here for you," Roger said with a glance around. "You shouldn't have come this far."

"Well, I did," Beverly said, "and I intend to go with you wherever you go. I'm not going back to the boat!"

"But——"

"It won't be any worse to go on with you," she said persuasively, "than to go all the way back alone! Don't say another word!" she commanded as he opened his mouth to protest. "I'm not going to leave you."

"But the others will be worried," he said. "Besides, we might get lost here in the native city. Neither of us is very familiar with it," he murmured.

Beverly shook her head. "No matter what you say, I am still going on. If Barney is in Shanghai I want to know where he is. Then we will have to get word to Larry somehow."

The Count sauntered across the street. Beverly and Jim followed at a discreet distance. A youngster came running from a shop so unexpectedly that he almost bowled Beverly over. She set him right side up and he ran off, disappearing in the throng.

"What was it he put in your pocket?" Roger asked as they hurried to catch up to the Count.

"My pocket?" Beverly asked in surprise.

"Oh, I'm getting to be a regular detective," he laughed. "When you bent over to pick him up he put something in your jacket pocket. I saw him."

"Another note!" Beverly exclaimed as her fingers extracted a bit of yellow paper.

"Read it," Roger commanded.

"It is in Larry's handwriting," she said, glancing at him significantly. "It says—'Go back to the boat while there is yet time! Don't you ever obey good advice? Go back!' " She looked up with a worried frown. "He seems to mean it."

"Of course he means it," Roger said. "But I wonder why he is so insistent upon it? A few hours shouldn't make any difference. I don't think anything more will happen to the yacht. As for us——"

"What could happen here on the street in broad daylight?" she asked.

"We don't know the Orient," Roger said wisely. "I wish you would go back, Beverly."

"Not without you," she said firmly.

"All right, then I'll go with you," he said with a sigh.

"Oh, Roger!" she exclaimed in disappointment. "You wouldn't—and let the Count get away? Why, this may be the only chance we will ever have of turning the tables on him. We've got to find out where he is going and if Black Barney is there. If we could somehow get hold of the other half of that map——"

Roger shook his head. "We will see where he goes and that is all. We are not going to invite any more trouble than we have to."

"All right," she submitted meekly.

Thereafter they walked for the most part in silence. It was growing dusk now. Long shadows were creeping over the streets. Some shops had lighted lamps on the interior. More than ever the unfamiliar faces on each side of them seemed to harbor no good for them. Hand in hand, to give each other courage, they went on.

Once the thought occurred to Beverly that the Count knew he was being followed and was deliberately leading them astray. He seemed to have no definite objective. He wandered in and out of shops aimlessly.

Beverly was getting impatient. At this rate they were getting nowhere. They might follow him all over Shanghai and still discover nothing. Barney might not be in Shanghai. The Count might only be stopping in the city momentarily before going on to join his fellow conspirators. These and other thoughts flitted through her mind as she walked beside Roger.

Roger, his tanned face set and a trifle grim, kept his eyes fixedly on the figure ahead. He felt he had a personal score to settle with the Count and Barney for kidnaping the girls and causing so much anxiety. He had never liked the Count, even when they met on a friendly basis in Switzerland and Paris. There had been something in the man he had always mistrusted. Now that mistrust had definitely crystallized into hatred. Part of Beverly's and Lenora's plea for action had entered his heart. The Count and Barney had been following them, threatening them, thwarting their plans, for so long that Roger was becoming anxious to put an end to it. He had a daring desire to follow the Count until he should come face to face with Black Barney! He wanted to see the man, to see the unknown terror who had been shadowing their days ever since they left Paris.

But between him and any such step stood Beverly. He could not take her into the midst of all the criminals. He could not permit her to take such a chance. But how to make her go back to the yacht? He knew she would not listen to anything he would say. In her way, she was as determined to meet Barney as he was. Still——

The Count disappeared around the corner of a building. Hurrying to catch up with him they saw him vanishing into a narrow alleyway. His movements were not aimless now. He walked quietly, speedily, to a small wooden door set in the expanse of wall. Without a backward glance he opened the door and went in.

"Now what?" Beverly asked her companion.

"Go back to the yacht and get Paul, Terry, and Jim. Bring them here. We'll find out if Barney is in there."

"I won't leave you," Beverly said. "Besides, suppose I go back and in the meantime the Count comes out and goes somewhere else? Or suppose it is merely another store? Let's go in and investigate ourselves."

"Oh, no!" Roger said firmly. "You are not going in!"

Beverly laughed. "If you want to come along, hurry up!"

She stepped past him into the alleyway.

"Wait! Beverly!"

Beverly laughed over her shoulder at him, but she did not come back. Roger had no course but to follow. He did so with a thrill of apprehension and excitement. He had done his best to dissuade her, but, since she could not be persuaded to return to the "Susabella", they would go on together.

Noiselessly, inch by inch, Roger opened the door through which the Count had gone, and they stepped inside. A dimly lighted corridor met them. A swinging oil lamp at the far end was the only radiance supplied. A tinkle of Chinese music and the buzz of conversation came from afar.

"Must be the back door to a chopsuey restaurant or something," Roger whispered in her ear.

Beverly nodded but did not reply. There was not a sound here, close to them. Two doors opened off the corridor and at the end was an aperture covered by a curtain on which was painted, in glowing colors, a hideous dragon who spurted flame and fire.

"W-what do we do n-now?" Beverly wanted to know.

Roger pushed back his hat and surveyed their position.

"Personally, I would like to know what is behind each of those doors and that curtain."

"Let's find out," Beverly suggested practically.

They moved forward slowly, treading as softly as possible. It might take only the merest sound to bring the Count and Barney rushing at them. Roger went first and Beverly kept close to him.

She had the queerest feeling. It was as though unseen eyes were watching them. She felt that they had been under observation since the very first moment they entered the place. Where had the Count disappeared? Was he at this moment congratulating himself on bringing them to this strange building? Had it all been a trap to lead them into Barney's stronghold?

"I don't l-like this," she murmured in a low voice.

"It's too quiet," he agreed. "As though they were waiting for us to find them."

"D-do you s-suppose——" Beverly began fearfully.

"Here's the first door. Quiet now!" Roger commanded.

The young American placed his ear against the panel and through the faint yellow lamplight they looked at each other and strained to hear a sound. Cautiously Roger opened the door a few inches. Nothing happened. Suddenly he flung it wide. Only a black, impenetrable darkness met them. Roger brought a box of matches from his pocket and took a step inside the room.

The flickering bit of flame showed that boxes and bales of miscellaneous food supplies were piled there. Nothing moved. The silence enveloped them like a cloak.

"Empty!" Roger said.

They closed the door and when it clicked softly behind them they jumped as though at a cannon shot and then grinned sheepishly at each other.

"Now for the other one," Roger said.

They moved on to the next door.

"Something tells me we shouldn't do this," Beverly whispered. "L-let's get out of here."

"Go back now?" Roger demanded. "Nope. We came to find the Count and see what he was doing. Now that we are here I want to see what kind of a place this is."

The second door showed a faint strip of light beneath it.

"S-someone must be in there," she said.

As before, they leaned against the door and listened. Only the faint sounds of revelry coming from the distance disturbed the night. There was not a sound from the room they contemplated entering.

Roger shrugged his shoulders and swung the door open. They did not step inside immediately, however. They viewed the scene with shrewd eyes.

It was a small room with no window and only the door by which they had entered. In the center was a roughly hewn table and on this were scattered papers, a book with a torn cover, a half-used yellow pencil, and a few Chinese coins. Overhead an oil lamp sent forth a smoky light. The only chair was the one behind the table. In the corners of the room were piled boxes whose contents they could not identify.

Beverly's eyes traveled rapidly over the scene, missing nothing. That the room had been recently occupied was evident, for a half-smoked cigarette, lying on the edge of the table, was still burning. But it was not this that her gaze rested on longest. Lying on top of the tattered book was a brown piece of paper, its edges badly frayed. From the doorway Beverly could see the crude lines which were drawn upon it.

"Roger! Look!" Beverly was past him and into the room. She had the slip of paper in her hand, was gazing at it intently. "It's the other half of the map!"

With a look behind him at the empty corridor, Roger shut the door and came to her side. He took the paper from her.

"It is that all right!" he agreed.

They studied it a moment in silence. It was the other half of the map which they had heard about so often. With this piece and their own, the destination of the treasure would be clearly indicated.

Roger looked up uneasily.

"This is too easy, Bev. I don't like it. There is a trick somewhere."

"Quite right, Mr. Garrett. There is a trick and it is mine."

Without turning, Beverly knew who was standing behind her. There was only one voice in China like that! The Count had led them straight to Black Barney. It had been as she thought—a trap into which they had obligingly walked.

The door had not opened. From where she stood she could watch it. Yet Barney was behind her! Was this the China of which they had read—mysterious and unknown, with sliding panels and hidden passageways?

"Good evening, Miss Gray."

So the Count had come, too, presumably to gloat over his victory. Beverly took another leisurely look at the map before she turned to confront them. Roger took a step closer to her and grasped her hand firmly in his.

"This must be Black Barney, alias a river pirate," he said easily.

"That's right," Barney said, seating himself in the only chair in the room.

The Count remained standing in the shadows. Behind him yawned an open section of the wall.

"What is it, a party?" Roger continued, noticing the Count.

"A party at which you are the honored guests," Barney nodded.

"Secret passages and sliding panels," Beverly said, walking to the wall and examining it.

"Charlie Wong's house is very old and very interesting," the Count agreed. "It will give me great pleasure to show you more of it."

"Some other time," Beverly said hastily, returning to Roger's side. "Why did you want us to come here?"

"It is a continuation of a little matter we started at my camp on the Si River," Barney said, leaning toward them. "Have you forgotten?"

Roger and Beverly remained silent.

"This time there will be no boat for you to escape in." His face grew dark with anger. "And no secret-agent white man to help you!"

He knew about Larry, then. Beverly wondered how he had found out about her friend. This time he was so sure there would be no one to come to their aid. Yet—Beverly remembered Larry's notes. If he knew where they were every minute, as his notes had indicated in their queer method of delivery, and he was well aware of Barney's presence in Shanghai, surely he would find some means to help them!

"I'll leave you alone for a little while," the Count

said and stepped back into the dark passageway. The section of the wall slid into place behind him.

"Suppose we get down to business," Barney suggested to the two young people left with him. "I am willing to offer you a safe return to your yacht and the other members of your party in return for what I want."

"Which is——" Roger said.

"The other half of this map." Barney tapped the torn piece of paper which Beverly had replaced upon the table.

"I haven't got it," Roger said defiantly.

"Perhaps not," Barney shrugged. "But one of your friends does have it. I want it!"

"Suppose you don't get it?" Roger asked. He sat on the edge of the table and grinned down at his archenemy in a most familiar manner.

"Then you probably will not see the yacht again," Barney said. "Charlie Wong's house is well-equipped to hide even a small army—let alone two people. Too, Charlie Wong has excellent facilities for transporting people into the interior, and China is a large place. When one is a stranger here it is so easy to become lost and perhaps wander into the hands of pirates—or fanatical tribes along the Mongolian Border."

Roger was about to make a fitting and insolent reply when the door through which they had entered burst abruptly open. The Count stood there. Behind him, in the corridor, two Chinamen were visible.

"Well?" Barney shot the word across the room.

"The rest of the party from the yacht are out in the big room," the Count said. "They have the Ambassador's daughter and a couple of naval officers with them."

"The fleet has landed and has the situation well in hand," Roger said flippantly.

Their friends! Naval officers? Beverly tried to fathom what it might mean. Surely they were not searching for them already! They could hardly even know she and Roger were in need of help. They could not know they were all in the same building!

"You should have known better than to try to keep us here," Roger said.

"What do they want?" Barney asked the Count.

"They are ordering dinner," the Count said. "I don't think they suspect anything but you never can tell——"

"Come," Barney said crisply and he and the Count left the room.

Roger and Beverly were alone. Roger strode to the door, but all chance of escape was blocked by a huge figure of a Chinaman standing on guard.

"If we could find the secret panel," Beverly suggested.

They surveyed the smooth expanse of wall. There was not a sign of anything out of the ordinary.

"It's hopeless," Roger said, shaking his head. "What are you doing?" he asked.

Beverly was bending over the table. She placed a

piece of paper over that of the map and hastily traced the broken lines.

"We probably won't have a chance to take the original," she explained. "But we will have a copy."

"Here they come," Roger said as footsteps sounded in the corridor. Rapidly he folded the paper and put it in his pocket.

"They are merely here on pleasure," Barney said, looming in the doorway. "They know nothing of you."

"Are you sure?" Beverly demanded.

"We will wait and find out," Barney said. "Meanwhile, we will continue our little chat in another room."

He crossed to the wall and as if by magic a panel flew back. He motioned Roger and Beverly to precede him.

Roger looked about him. He knew if once he or Beverly entered any of the maze of passages in this queer building there was little chance of their getting out again. Barney was watching him with a half smile. At the door stood the Count and two of the Chinese waiters from the restaurant outside.

"Do not be rash, Mr. Garrett," Barney said. "There is no chance for you to escape."

Beverly exchanged a hopeless glance with Roger. Silently she turned and stepped into the passageway. Roger followed and behind him came Barney. The panel slid shut and all around them was a darkness too dense to penetrate.

"Oh, Roger——" Beverly whispered hopelessly.

"Keep your chin up," Roger whispered. "If we could only get word to Jim somehow!"

"This way, Mr. Garrett and Miss Gray!" Barney's voice sounded through the darkness and echoed hollowly. His footsteps led off to the right. There was no course but for them to follow.

Beverly shivered. They never dreamed, that morning, when they had left the yacht so blithe and gay that they might never see it again. They had no idea they would ever be prisoners in a place like this. Deliberately, the Count had led them into ambush. They should not have followed him. They should not have been so blind!

But there was no use in lamenting what they had done. What could they do now was the question. Alone, unarmed, in the den of a group of criminals. They could not attempt and accomplish an escape. They might attempt it, but they would soon be overpowered. Their position here was even more hopeless than hers and Shirley's had been in the pirate camp. There they had had friends—Larry and Woo Fong.

They were descending steps now, Roger's arm supporting her so she did not stumble. Barney went on ahead. Behind them they could hear a queer shuffling sound, made by the sandals of a Chinaman, probably. It gave Beverly a shivery feeling. They did not move very fast, feeling their way in the darkness.

"If this is used so much why don't you provide

lamps?" Roger demanded as he stumbled over the last step.

"It is not used often," Barney said with a dry chuckle. "There was a man murdered at this spot only a month ago. A very opportune spot; no one could hear his cries."

Beverly felt as if an icy hand had grasped hold of her heart. Where would all this end? Could they ever hope to escape? Where was Barney taking them? What was that? A voice! A voice was speaking out of the darkness. An American voice! A familiar voice!

"You are wrong, Black Barney," the voice said, and Beverly could picture the smiling face of the owner. "Someone did hear his cries. Someone who has been on your trail for a long time, Barney.

"Tomorrow," the voice continued, "you will be behind bars, in prison, Barney, where you should have been long ago. Together, you and Charlie Wong will stand trial for all the crimes—smuggling, robbery, murder, kidnaping, and all the other things on record. You cannot escape this time."

Beverly became conscious of the fact that Roger was squeezing her hand so hard it hurt unbearably. She could feel his lips at her ear.

"When Larry finishes talking," Roger said, "I am going to jump upon Barney. Take this." He put into her hand what felt like a heavy club. "I picked it up a little while back. You stop whoever is coming behind us."

"I'll stop them!" Beverly promised breathlessly and felt the weight of the club.

This while Barney had been silent, stricken dumb with astonishment at the voice that came from the darkness. Now he found voice and shouted defiance.

"Come out, whoever you are! You cannot stop me! All the police in Shanghai couldn't find me in here! I'll escape yet and someday I'll find you—whoever you are. And when I do——"

Barney never had the chance to finish his threat. Roger leaped with all the agility, speed, and force he had displayed in many a college football game. A second more and they were rolling on the floor, struggling, battering at each other.

Beverly heard running feet. In the darkness she could not see who it was, but instinct told her it was no friend. She swung the club forcefully. It struck something soft and yielding. She heard a grunt and imagined that someone fell to the ground. But more running feet were coming along the corridor now. Anyone within the secret passage at the time must have heard the racket Roger and Barney were making.

Beverly longed to go to Roger's aid. The club was strong in her hands. She felt a murderous impulse to smash something with it. She owed Black Barney something and at that moment, if she could have known which of the two figures struggling on the floor was the pirate chief, Barney would have felt the full impact of the club. As it was, she could not strike at the figures for fear of hitting Roger.

Too, there were more pressing details. Another figure came flying to the scene. Beverly waved the club, not knowing or caring who or what she hit. But this time she was not so fortunate. Strong hands grasped her and the club was wrenched away. She was picked up bodily and her captor started at a light trot away from the scene.

"Roger!" Beverly cried, and then fought madly to free herself. She couldn't call upon Roger now. He had his hands full. She must try to get free!

Roger heard that cry and it inspired him afresh. Fighting desperately he suddenly felt his opponent's hold slacken. Soon Barney was lying on the floor and Roger was standing in silence over him. Other figures were on the scene. Still, strangely enough, no one lighted a match or lamp to illumine the proceedings. Roger backed against the wall and flattened himself there. He did not hear a sound now from Beverly. Perhaps she had fainted. That was a logical conclusion and the safest course for him was to wait. The sound of running feet sent the new arrivals off hotfoot down the corridor. Roger came away from the wall.

"Beverly!" he cried softly. He searched in his pockets for matches but he had none. In the darkness he felt around with his hands. Suddenly he touched a form, the clothes were soft silk. This was Beverly. He picked the girl up in his arms and started back the way they had come with Barney. In the blackness he stumbled many times but he did not stop. He must get Beverly out of here. If only this passage opened onto the outside.

He came to the steps they had descended and stopped. Perhaps it was imagination. No, there was a cool sweetness in the air here. A draft of air from the outside was clearly felt. He put his precious burden down upon the floor and felt along the wall. There was nothing but damp earth on one side. He crawled into a narrow space beneath the stairs. Success! Here was a door built into the wall. He knew it must be a door by the air that entered along a narrow slit down one side, yet his exploring fingers could find no way to open it.

Desperately he searched, knowing he could not waste any time. It would not be long before the pirates would discover their fallen leader and be after him and Beverly. They must get out now while he had time. Where was Larry? If only he were here to help!

Roger stepped back in disgust. The wall was perfectly smooth. The door presumably had a catch on the outside—not in here! He turned to further his search in other directions when his foot touched something small and hard on the floor. He pressed, heard a faint click, and the sought-for door opened outward into the night air.

Cautiously Roger put his head out and looked around. It was a narrow alley and deserted, luckily!

He went back and a moment later he brought Beverly out into the little street.

Here the moonlight faintly illumined the space between the houses. He knelt beside the one he had brought out of the den of the pirates and closed the door behind him. Only when his only means of re-entering the house was lost to him did he notice his mistake.

This was not Beverly he had rescued! The yellow face and slanting eyes, the silken jacket with its picture of a dragon, did not belong to her. He had carried one of the pirates to safety and left Beverly in there!

CHAPTER XVII

Capture

BEVERLY'S CAPTOR ran swiftly, easily avoiding any pitfalls. There could be no doubt that he was familiar with this corridor. Not once did he slacken his pace or his hold upon her. The sounds of struggle were left behind them.

Beverly tried to retain some sense of direction but it was impossible. This man must have eyes like a cat, able to see in the dark, to be so sure-footed. Beverly remained quiet, docile in his arms. She was waiting for his grasp to loosen, then she would try again to escape. She had fought desperately at first, biting, kicking, scratching, but with a quiet strength and firmness he had thwarted all her attempts to elude him. She had been practically helpless. Yet her mind was scheming, planning, hoping——

When it seemed they had come a long way and the sounds of Roger's fight could no longer be heard, they left the corridor and entered a small room. Beverly's captor set her down, lighted a candle to relieve the darkness, and went out, closing the door behind him. She heard a lock click home. She was a prisoner.

The room was bare of furnishings. The candle was stuck in a hollow in the wall and its meager light scarcely penetrated to the four corners of the room.

With a shudder Beverly tried to rid herself of the vision of her captor. What new terror was this? The Chinaman who had brought her here was, to her way of thinking, far more horrifying than Black Barney or the Count. She saw again with startling clearness the black, matted hair, the scarred face, the leering grin, and the murderous knife sticking in his belt.

She tried to open the door but it was useless. The lock was strong enough to resist her efforts. Back against the panels she surveyed the room, fighting to remain calm and cool. There must be a way out of this! Perhaps Roger would emerge victorious from the battle and come to rescue her. Perhaps Larry would come out of his hiding place. That was her only hope.

It seemed incredulous that anything of this sort should happen in such modern times. Many people had told her that the Orient is strange. Many things happen there that cannot rationally be explained or corrected. Places such as this, built in the times of the ancient East, still exist behind the veneer of civilization. Modern education, modern science, modern manners—all these cannot reach to every corner of the Orient.

" 'East is East and West is West and never the twain shall meet!' " she reminded herself.

Was it possible that Jim and Shirley and the others were in Charlie Wong's restaurant enjoying a delicious dinner while all the time this was happening beneath their very feet? Wasn't there some way to reach them? Oh, if only she could get out of this room!

Beverly took the candle from its niche in the wall and walked slowly about the narrow confines of the room. The walls all seemed secure, no sliding panels here. There was no hollow echo when she rapped upon them. And then she saw it! A trap door! She took hold of the small ring and pulled with all her might. It was heavy, but she lifted the door. Holding the candle down into the open space Beverly could see a flight of steps leading downward. What should she do? Remain here indefinitely, or take her chances with what she might encounter if she went through the trap door into the subcellar?

She remembered her captor and shivered. Certainly she could not remain here! Anything would be better than waiting for that man to come and unlock the door!

Without more ado Beverly let herself down into the yawning black hole. She had a moment of hesitation about closing the trap door after her, but she finally concluded it might help to delay any pursuit.

There was only a short flight of steps leading down to another earthen floor. She reached it with a great

deal of thanksgiving, for the ladder had been rickety.
The candle did not serve to illumine the room, in
which she now found herself, sufficiently for her to
be able to distinguish every detail. She did note that
it was deserted, however, and this helped to steady
her a little. She moved forward silently, casting
frightened glances about at the silent walls. Once
there was a slight noise and her heart leaped into her
throat as a rat scurried across the path of candlelight.

Never, never, as long as she lived, would she forget
this night and her visit to Shanghai! She had longed
for new adventures, new scenes—well, she was getting them! Wait until Charlie Blaine read this ac-
count of her visit to Shanghai! He probably would
not believe a word of it.

What was that? She crouched breathlessly against
the wall, looking back the way she had come. Footsteps! There was the bright beam of an electric
torch. The white light danced over the walls behind
her. Beverly stood still, holding her breath, lest the
merest sound betray her position to her pursuer.
Could he see the light from her candle?

Searching for a place to hide or means to escape
Beverly fled forward blindly. Once she stumbled and
fell headlong. She was up in a moment, poised for
flight while she listened for the man behind her. Her
candle was out now, snuffed into blackness when she
fell. The blackness ahead was impenetrable, hiding
a hundred terrors, while behind her came the horrifying Chinaman!

The flashlight danced closer to her this time, coming nearer and nearer as the footsteps sounded on the floor, rattling stones, and echoing hollowly.

She wouldn't go back with that Chinaman! Beverly turned and fled indiscreetly. The blackness ahead could hold no more terrors than she had already experienced! With no candle to shed its light before her, no way of knowing where she was going, she found it difficult progress. Once she bumped into the wall when the corridor turned abruptly. But she did not stop. Her heart sounded like thunder in her ears. She did not know where she was going and she scarcely cared. All she wanted to do was get as far away as possible from the man pursuing her.

Once she stopped to look back. She fancied he was almost upon her. Recklessly she fled the spot. In the darkness she could not see what she had come upon, but suddenly she felt herself falling—falling—falling—and then there was nothing but empty space.

Roger got to his feet and called himself all manners of an idiot. If he had done a hundred stupid things in his life this was the prize one of them all. Rescuing a pirate from his own gang! Where was Beverly? What had become of her? How could he get back in and find her? What could he do singlehanded against all the others?

His brain worked like lightning. He remembered the Count saying that the rest of the party from the "Susabella" were in Charlie Wong's restaurant. He

hoped they were still there! Rapidly he went down
the alleyway to the street. He had no choice but to
leave the pirate outside the secret door. The man
would have to take care of himself; Roger had more
pressing matters on his mind.

He did not notice that the people he passed going
into Charlie Wong's chophouse looked at him
strangely. He did not know what damage the fight in
the dark had caused to his appearance. His suit was
torn and dirty. His face was scratched and his right
eye was rapidly swelling. He could feel these things
but, without a mirror, did not realize what a startling
revelation his appearance would be to his friends.

He stopped in the doorway of the eating place and
waved away the waiter that approached him and
bowed. He saw the others at a large table, laughing
hilariously, having the time of their lives. There were
several strangers, including three naval officers. Too,
he recognized Anthony Anton as he made his way
toward them.

Lenora stared at him open-mouthed. Paul and Lois
did not immediately recognize him. Shirley jumped
up with a little cry of consternation. Jim got up and
pushed Roger into his chair, asking abruptly:

"Where's Beverly?"

"What have you been doing?" Lenora demanded.
"Cleaning the streets?"

"Cleaning a secret passageway and using Black
Barney as a broom," Roger said, rubbing the bruised
knuckles of his right hand.

"I say, old man, tell us what happened," Terry said.

The strangers in the party—Lottie, two other girls, three young men, and the naval officers—exchanged glances with Anthony Anton. All leaned forward intently.

"I haven't got time for a lot of explanations," Roger said tersely. "All I can tell you now is that Black Barney and the Count are down in the cellar of this place and Beverly is there—somewhere. I came to get help—we've got to go down there and find her!"

"Do you boys like to fight?" Lenora demanded of the navy men.

"Rather!" the three exclaimed in unison.

The other three men whom the group had met here in Charlie Wong's when they came from the yacht added their approval of the suggestion, as did Anthony Anton.

"We'll clean the place thoroughly," Paul said crisply. "Let's go!"

"What'll we do?" Lenora demanded.

"Go back to the yacht!" Terry replied immediately.

"Get the police," Roger added. "Send them here. We'll probably need them."

"Be careful, won't you?" Shirley begged of Roger.

In a body the young men got up and followed Roger outside. They went to the alleyway where Beverly and Roger had first entered the building.

They found the same door but this time it was locked.

"Break it in!" Jim said practically.

Three of them put their shoulders to the door and it finally gave under their combined weight.

The eleven, under the leadership of Roger, burst into the building. He went immediately to the room where they had found the second half of the map and where Barney had confronted them. They were just in time to witness the pirate chief himself putting a match to the precious piece of paper. The map burned rapidly, and as he saw them and dropped it to flee they sprang forward.

"Hold him, Mr. Anton!" Roger shouted.

The explorer obligingly knelt upon the fallen pirate and grinned down at the scowling face.

"Take it easy, old chap; your running days are over."

"At least you can't have the map," Black Barney said. "I know what was on it but you will never know now."

The second half of the map lay a charred bit of ashes on the floor beside him.

"You may know what was on it," Mr. Anton agreed, "but you will have small chance to use that knowledge in prison."

Meanwhile Roger and Jim and the three naval men had plunged into the secret passageway. They reached the stairs and descended to the lower cellar. Silently now they moved forward. Ahead of them they caught sight of a flickering light. It disappeared after a moment and when they reached the spot they found it was a room and into it had gone four of the wickedest-looking men any of them had ever seen. The pirates were discussing something in their native tongue and were not aware of the presence of the Americans, until the door was slammed shut and locked.

The three naval officers mounted guard over the pirates while Roger and Jim went on in search of Beverly.

"Shshshsh," Roger warned suddenly. "Someone's coming!"

The two flattened themselves against the wall, waiting, waiting for whoever was coming to identify themselves.

"I've got him!" Roger shouted exultantly and hurled himself upon the man.

Jim flung himself forward, too. Both of the young Americans landed on the unsuspecting man and bore him to the ground.

"Don't!" Beverly cried, tugging at Roger's arm.

He was so surprised he stopped and looked up. Jim rose to his feet.

"All right, Beverly?" he asked anxiously.

"Yes," Beverly acknowledged, "except for some scratches and bruises I got running away from Larry."

"Larry!" exclaimed Roger and looked down at the man on the ground.

The light from Larry's flashlight lent a faint radiance to the scene.

"Yes, Larry!" that individual said laboriously, getting to his feet. "You almost smashed me flatter than a pancake."

Roger surveyed his friend from head to foot. Larry had proved to be the "terrible" pirate from whom Beverly fled so hurriedly. When he took her to that deserted room he had locked her in for her own protection and, not stopping to reveal his identity, fled back to help Roger. There, he found that young man had already escaped, so he had gone back to Beverly, only to find her fleeing from him in nameless terror.

"Even your best friend wouldn't recognize you!" Jim declared to Larry.

"I've been wearing this for two weeks off and on," Larry said. "Now to get out of here! Take Beverly back, will you? I've got Count Alexis locked up in a room."

"We've got Black Barney and four of his men," Roger informed him. "What'll we do with them?"

"The police will be here any minute," Larry said. "I sent for them."

"So did we," Jim laughed. "We'll have the whole force down on our ears. Let's get out of here."

Up in the room with Black Barney, Roger and Jim decided to stay with the explorer until the police came.

"You go out and if the girls are still waiting, tell

them we have the situation well in hand," Roger told her.

Accordingly, Beverly went out into the night as swiftly as she could. The girls were en masse in front of the restaurant.

Shirley pounced upon Beverly eagerly. In her anxiety she was shaking Beverly without realizing it.

"Roger? Is Roger all right? He isn't hurt——"

"Roger?" Beverly asked in surprise. "He's all right——"

"Are you sure, Beverly? You're sure——"

Beverly tried to grasp the significance of Shirley's anxiety. Both Jim and Roger had been in the Chinese stronghold. Shirley was mostly concerned with Roger's welfare. Then it was Roger for whom Shirley cared——

"B-but I thought——" Beverly began in amazement. "You're in love with Roger!"

Shirley nodded, color staining her cheeks.

"And all the time I thought——" Beverly said.

The police chose that moment to arrive on the scene. Everything became excitement and uproar, until finally the tired Americans could again turn their attention to the "Susabella" and comfortable cabins.

CHAPTER XVIII

All Aboard!

"Quiet!" Lenora shouted.

"Why?" Lois wanted to know impertinently.

It was the next morning. The party was at breakfast and they had all been avidly discussing the previous night's excitement.

"What I want to know is what do we do now?" Lenora demanded. "If Black Barney burned the map what will we do?"

"He burned it," Roger agreed. "But not until after Beverly had made a copy of it and we both memorized most of it."

"What? Then we still have a chance of finding the treasure? Goody! Goody!" Lenora wiggled excitedly in her seat.

"Can you put your half onto our half?" Lois asked. "Do it now and see what it looks like."

Jim brought out his half and Beverly hers. What she did not have time to put on her rough sketch last night she and Roger drew in now. The others hung attentively over their shoulders.

"I told Larry about this last night," Roger said, "and he wants to join the hunt. He says he knows a man who would be a valuable guide for us, too. So I suggested that he bring him along."

"The four words on the back of our half read Fiji, inland, Temple, and pillar. Put Barney's half with it and it reads—'Northeast of Fiji, Fifty yards inland, ruin of Temple, and second pillar,'" said Jim thoughtfully.

"The Temple and the pillar must be what the X's mark," Paul surmised.

"If it is the ruin of a temple, Anthony Anton should be interested," Lenora said brightly. "Doesn't he mess around in those sort of things?"

"Let's ask him," Shirley proposed. "If we discover any relics of real value we wouldn't know it. But if he was there—he's an authority——"

"Have you got it all together?" Jim asked of Roger and Beverly.

"I believe we have," Beverly nodded slowly.

"Hello, everybody!" Larry appeared in the doorway.

"We were so interested in the map we didn't hear anyone arrive," Terry said.

"I've brought company," Larry continued. "Mr. Anton and the man I was telling you about, Roger— Shanghai Pete."

"Shanghai Pete! What a name!" Lenora exclaimed.

Behind Larry entered Mr. Anton and, to their surprise, a small, wiry man with a parrot perched on his shoulder.

"John!" Lenora and Lois exclaimed.

"Pretty girl!" squawked the parrot.

"The man we saw at Kin Yang's!" Beverly and Shirley said together.

Larry nodded. "Shanghai Pete and I have been working together. I missed him that day at Kin Yang's and he sent the parrot on board the 'Susabella' to deliver a note to me. John is often used for that. When Pete wanted his bird back we had to steal him from Lenora," he grinned. "I might as well explain, too, that Pete helped me a lot in delivering those warning notes yesterday when I was trying to keep you away from Charlie Wong's because of Black Barney."

The mention of Barney's name brought the discussion of Charlie Wong's mysterious house to the fore again. All of them tried to talk at once and the room was filled with the hubbub.

Later on, when some of them had quieted down, attention was turned to the map again. Anthony Anton was very much interested in it. Eagerly he agreed to join the hunt for the buried treasure.

"And Shanghai Pete will be our guide," Larry proposed. "He knows the islands around Fiji; he knows what sort of things we'll need."

"Hurrah!"

Lois and Lenora danced about in glee.

"On to the treasure!" Lenora cried brightly.

So, with new adventures beckoning just ahead, let us leave Beverly Gray and her friends to again join them in Beverly Gray on a Treasure Hunt, when we will discover to what the map did eventually lead them.

THE BEVERLY GRAY
MYSTERY STORIES